NANTUCKET HOMES

PAMELA M. KELLEY

PIPING PLOVER PRESS

ISBN 978-1-953060-31-0

INTRODUCTION

It's Fall on Nantucket--and change is in the air!

There's a new arrival to the island. Kay Johnson, a widow, was a friend of Lisa's mother and is like an aunt to Lisa. Kay is excited to relax and enjoy Nantucket—she's already signed up for a Needlepoint class. She's not at all looking for romance, but she is happy to make a new friend in neighbor Walter Sturgess, a widower.

When the story begins, Walter's son Travis, CEO of a tech company he founded in Silicon Valley, and his four-year-old daughter, Sophie, are living with Walter until Travis's new home is ready for them to move in.

That new home is being built by Chase Hodges, Lisa's son, and is located on the ocean, next to the home where Victoria grew up--and is now living temporarily with her parents, since she and Todd—her long-term boyfriend and fiancé, broke up.

When she sees Travis for the first time in many years, Victoria realizes he is in a similar place, since his divorce. She didn't even recognize Travis at first. He had to remind her that they'd once dated in high school, before she dumped him for Todd, the star quarterback. Travis is all grown-up now, but even if she was interested in dating, Victoria has never been anxious to have children, let alone take on someone else's.

Meanwhile, Lisa's online food business was growing steadily until recently when she discovered several competitors making copycat lobster quiches and it is affecting her sales. Marley, her marketing advisor, studies the situation and advises what Lisa thinks is a questionable suggestion- but she's willing to give it a try.

Chase and Beth are also dealing with some unwelcome competition, when Chase discovers that he's losing new business bids to an upstart construction company--that is underbidding by such an amount that Chase can't imagine how they are making a profit.

And speaking of babies, Victoria isn't the only one who isn't sure she wants to have children. Now that she and Tyler are married, Kristen has been thinking a lot about that as well.

Come back to Nantucket and see what all of your old friends are up to. If you like romantic women's fiction

and family focused stories you might find yourself addicted to this series. Be sure to start with book one, The Nantucket Inn.

*K*ay Johnson waved as she drove her baby-blue Mini Cooper off the ferry and spotted Lisa and Rhett waiting on Nantucket Wharf. Kay had been Lisa's mother's best friend and was like an aunt. Lisa had invited her to attend her small wedding when she and Rhett married, but Kay was on a trip of a lifetime, traveling across Europe with several of her best friends. She'd visited as soon as she returned and had such a lovely time that she'd decided to return soon after and booked a two-month stay at the inn.

It was always bittersweet when Lisa first saw Kay as she reminded her of her mother, who'd been gone now for many years. Kay was in her early seventies and tiny. She was barely five feet tall and maybe a hundred pounds. Her hair was short, gray that she dyed blonde, and it curled every which way, giving her an impish look, which was strengthened when she smiled and her hazel eyes twinkled. She had an upbeat, sunny personality and was always fun to be around. Lisa was looking forward to spending time with her. She hadn't wanted to charge her for the room, but Kay had insisted.

"I'm going to stay for at least two months. If I'm paying, I won't feel so bad about staying that long."

Lisa had finally agreed but insisted on a deeply discounted family and friends rate.

"It's so good to see you," Lisa said as Kay pulled up to them with her window rolled down. "How was the ride over?"

"Went by in a flash. Got myself a glass of chardonnay and by the time I finished sipping it and enjoying the view, we arrived."

"It's good to see you again." Rhett said as Lisa got into the passenger side of Kay's car while Rhett walked back to where he'd parked and would meet them at the house.

Kay chatted away as they drove, catching Lisa up on her family. Kay had one child, Tony, that was high up in the military and stationed overseas in Japan.

"He says he'll be there another five years until he retires. But it wouldn't surprise me if he stays there longer. His life is there now and her family, too." Tony's wife, Luanne, was Japanese and their two adult children lived nearby. Lisa suspected Kay was probably right. She felt for her. It must be hard to be so far away from her family. They came back to the States when they could, and Kay went there often, too, but it wasn't the same. Lisa felt fortunate that her four adult children were all on Nantucket and that she saw them often.

When they reached the house, Rhett pulled up right behind them and brought Kay's suitcases up to her room. Lisa chose Abby's old room for Kay, as it was decorated in soft yellows and blues and had the prettiest view of the ocean.

"Are you hungry? I hope you'll join us for dinner? It's nothing fancy, just meatloaf and mashed potatoes, but I'd love to catch up with you."

Kay smiled. "Of course. I'd love that."

"Come on in then. It's warming on the stove." Lisa led the way into the kitchen. She poured a glass of chardonnay for Kay and two glasses of a red blend for her and Rhett.

"I'm just going to make some garlic bread and then we can eat." Lisa sliced a big loaf of Italian bread in half length-wise, spread softened butter on both halves, then sprinkled minced garlic and chopped parsley over it, put the two halves together, wrapped it all in tin foil and put it in the oven to bake.

Fifteen minutes later, they sat down to eat meatloaf, mashed potatoes, roasted asparagus, and crusty garlic bread.

"Lisa, this is wonderful. It brings back memories. I used to make this for Al. It was his favorite meal. It's been two years this month." Her eyes took on a damp shine as she spoke of her husband. Lisa reached over and gave her hand a squeeze.

"I'm so sorry, Kay. I know you must miss him still."

"Every day," she admitted. "But it's not as hard as it was the first year. You know how that is. Now, it just hits me once in a while, when something makes me think of him."

Lisa nodded. "I know. It's hard." Lisa hadn't thought she'd ever be interested in dating again, after she lost her husband Brian to cancer a few years back. That first year had been so hard. And she'd had to find a way to support herself after discovering that most of her savings were gone, thanks to Brian's secret gambling habit. But once she'd found a solution, to turn her waterfront house into a bed-and-breakfast, she'd also unexpectedly found love when she met Rhett—her first guest. She liked to tease him that he was the guest that came and never left. And she couldn't be happier about it.

Kay looked around the table at Lisa and Rhett and smiled. "I'm really not too sad anymore. I miss Al, but we had a wonderful life together and many happy memories. Now, I'd like to focus on making more memories. I'm looking forward to enjoying my time here and exploring the island. I've already signed up for needlepoint classes. The first one starts on Tuesday. I looked it up online."

Lisa laughed. "That's marvelous! You'll enjoy the classes. The woman that owns the shop is a retired teacher, and she loves needlepoint. I took the class a while back, and it was fun."

"There's a senior center I want to check out too. And I thought about maybe volunteering with the food pantry. I do that at home."

"Abby is active with the food pantry. I'll tell her you'd like to help and she can put you on the schedule while you're here."

Kay smiled. "Good! I like to keep busy. I'm looking forward to my morning walks along the beach, too."

When they finished eating, Kay yawned and immediately apologized. "How rude of me. I think the day of traveling and this delicious food has caught up with me. I expect to sleep well tonight."

Rhett laughed. "Did you save room for dessert? Lisa went to the Italian bakery earlier today."

Kay's eyes lit up. "You did? I'm pretty full, but I could probably manage a little bit of dessert."

"Good, because I picked up the most delicious tiramisu for us." Lisa quickly cleared the dishes and set the tiramisu in the middle of the table, along with a serving spoon and three plates, so they could all help themselves. Kay took a small portion, and after she finished, immediately went back for more.

"This is so good. I should have cut a bigger slice. But you never know."

Lisa laughed. "Have all you want. We don't get it often. But for special occasions, when we see our favorite people, it's perfect."

"Thank you. I had a moment of second-guessing myself this morning. Wondering if I was crazy to head off to Nantucket for a few months. I've never done anything like this—other than the trip to Europe with the girls. But I've been thinking about this trip ever since I visited you both after you got married. And now that I'm here, I couldn't be more excited. I know it was the right decision."

"Well, we're certainly glad that you are here. I'll have a girls' night soon, so you can visit with some of my friends and tomorrow afternoon, all the kids are coming for Sunday dinner, and they're all excited to see you, too."

After dinner, Kay said goodnight to Lisa and Rhett and made her way up to her room. It was up a short flight of stairs and though it was too dark now to see the view, Kay knew she would enjoy it when she woke in the morning. She fought back another yawn as she unpacked and put her clothes away in the chest of drawers. She knew that Nantucket weather, like all of New England, could vary wildly from cool one day to warm the next, so she'd made sure to bring layers and sweaters she could add or take off.

She hadn't mentioned it at dinner because she wanted to keep the mood light, but the recent months had brought even more changes to Kay's life. One of her best friends had suffered a stroke and was having a slow recovery. Once she was better, her husband was planning to relocate them to Arizona, where the weather was better for both of them. And her other best friend, Judy, had just made the move to Florida a permanent one. She was moving into an in-law apartment at her oldest son's home in Tampa. The changes left Kay feeling very alone. Even though she still had plenty of friends, they weren't her best friends and everywhere she went, she was reminded that nothing was the same anymore.

Coming to Nantucket was a chance to explore and focus on something new. After Nantucket, she thought she might spend a few months down south in the Charleston area. She'd visited there once and had always wanted to go back. She and Al had always been careful with money and as a result, she had a healthy bank account.

Her son had encouraged her to spend some of it and do the things she'd always dreamed of doing, traveling and seeing the world. Nantucket was the first step, and though she'd had a moment of doubt earlier in the day, she was at peace with her decision and knew she was where she was supposed to be, for now.

2

"*I* can't believe I agreed to do this. Let's just skip it and head to B-ACK Yard BBQ with everyone," Victoria said.

But Taylor, who sat at the desk right behind her, shook her head. "Absolutely not. We're doing this. I'll go tell Blake that we'll meet them all there. It won't take us long." She got up before Victoria could say a word and ran to her boyfriend, Blake's, office. He and his father, who was semi-retired, owned the newspaper where Taylor and Victoria worked. A moment later, Blake walked out the door with Emily from sales and Joe, the most senior reporter, who was also their immediate supervisor.

Taylor returned and sat back down at her desk.

"Okay, let's do this. Pull up the form."

Victoria did as instructed and her screen filled with the homepage for the Perfect Match online dating site.

"Have you really done this before?" Victoria asked. Taylor was madly in love with Blake and as far as Victoria knew, hadn't dated anyone else since she'd moved to

Nantucket. Victoria hadn't thought she'd ever be in this position. When she'd moved home to Nantucket, she'd been engaged. Todd was working at his family's real estate company. She'd left a good job at the Boston Herald to move home. And it had been fine, until Todd decided that he no longer wanted to get married, broke up with her and moved to Alaska. To say it was a shock was an understatement.

Victoria had done a lot of soul-searching since then, trying to make sense of it. She and Todd had dated all through high school and then college. Everyone had assumed they'd be together forever, including Victoria. But Todd had gently explained that he just wasn't sure what he wanted and that he'd proposed because it was the logical thing to do after dating for so long. She'd been furious at first. Mostly because it was so unexpected. She and Todd had always gotten along so well. But if she was being honest with herself, she knew that, while there was a great friendship between them, she hadn't felt butterflies with Todd in a long time.

She'd wondered about it now and then but had told herself it was normal when a couple was together as long as they had been—but maybe it wasn't normal? It would be nice to feel butterflies again with someone. If that was possible. Since she and Todd had broken up almost six months ago, she hadn't gone on a single date. A few guys had shown some interest, but she hadn't been ready yet. She still wasn't totally sure that she was ready to get back out there.

But Taylor thought it was a good idea and Victoria trusted her. They'd had a bit of a rocky start—which was entirely Victoria's fault. She hadn't exactly welcomed Taylor with open arms when she joined the paper a few weeks after Victoria. But as they'd gotten to know each other, they'd developed a friendship. And when Todd ended things, Taylor had been so supportive.

"Yes, of course I have. Everyone does it. I met some great guys in Charleston that way."

Victoria took a deep breath. "Okay then, I guess I'm as ready as I'll ever be."

"I created a profile for you. Look it over and let me know what you think. We can change anything." Taylor pulled up the profile she'd created and waited for Victoria's response.

The headline read, Never a dull moment, which made Victoria smile.

Fun-loving, curious and compassionate thirty-something seeks a smart, active partner for new adventures. Love the beach, live music and good food—though I don't cook—extra bonus points if you do. Just amicably ended a long-term relationship, so looking to take things slow and see where they go.

Victoria laughed when she finished reading it. "You really nailed me. Do you think it's a good idea to be that honest? I mean, to volunteer that kind of information?"

Taylor nodded. "Blake has a saying, 'get ugly early'... in other words, show people who you really are and if they are attracted still, then you have something to build on."

"I suppose that makes sense. If anyone responds."

"They will. We need to add some pictures. You look cute today. That's a great outfit. I'll get a full shot of you outside and a few headshots now."

Victoria was wearing one of her favorite outfits, a bright pink sleeveless sweater that highlighted her toned arms. She worked hard on those arms. Since the breakup, she'd started going back to the gym regularly and taking classes that combined weights with cardio. Because she was trying to get her mind off the breakup, her focus was better than usual, and though she wasn't overweight before, she was now toned and her clothes fit better.

Taylor had her stand by a window where the light was better and took several pictures from the shoulders up. They tried a few smiling and a few without and agreed that smiling was the way to go. She stepped outside and Taylor positioned her so that the distant view of the harbor was behind her and she took a full-length picture. Victoria was wearing an old pair of jeans that were slightly faded and flattering. Taylor seemed thrilled with the pictures and quickly uploaded them to the site.

"Okay, your pictures are up. Now, what do you want your username to be?"

Victoria hadn't a clue. "Victoria?"

Taylor frowned. "It's probably a good idea to use something that is a bit more vague, just to be careful. Victoria's not that common a name. How about Nantucket Original?"

"Sure. That works." She had been born on Nantucket, so it fit and would be easy to remember. She handed Taylor a credit card, and she quickly finished creating the account.

Victoria suddenly had second thoughts about putting the pictures up, though.

"Can we hold off on the pictures? Wait and see if anyone responds just to the profile? And if I like theirs? I can always send the pictures later, right? Too many people know me here. It might be weird."

Taylor bit her lip. "Well, you could. But you'll get way more responses with your pictures."

"I think I want to wait and ease into it."

Taylor nodded and made a few clicks.

"You're good to go now. The profile should be live in twenty-four hours. Be sure to check it often and keep me posted."

Victoria grinned. "Will do. Thank you. I have to admit, I'm a little nervous about this."

"Don't be nervous. It will be fun!"

3

"*D*addy, read it again!" The sweet baby voice and big gray eyes looking into his made it impossible for Travis Sturgess to say no. Even though it was long past her bedtime. If four-year-old Sophie, the most important person in his life, wanted her father to read *Fancy Nancy* again, he would do it. He pulled his daughter closer, and she snuggled against him. Her soft blonde curls tickled his chin, and he smiled as he flipped to the beginning of the book and began reading out loud again.

But this time, he only made it a few pages before Sophie fell fast asleep. Travis waited a few minutes to make sure she stayed asleep, then scooped her up, brought her into her bedroom and tucked her into bed. When he returned to the living room, his father raised his eyebrows from where he sat rocking in his favorite chair.

"She has you wrapped around her finger."

Travis laughed. "That she does. You want a beer? I'm going to grab one." He headed toward his father's kitchen. He and Sophie were staying temporarily until his house was ready to move in. They were still a few months away from it being finished.

"Sure, why not? Just one though. You know I never have more than that."

Travis smiled as he pulled two beers out of the refrigerator, opened them, and handed one to his father. His father rarely drank, though since Travis had moved in, he sometimes joined him and when he did, it was always just one.

They sipped their beers in comfortable silence. His father wasn't a big talker, and that was fine with Travis. It had been a long day, and he was tired. But just as he was about to break the silence, his father surprised him by talking first.

"You ever try online dating?"

Travis laughed. "Sure, but not in a few years."

His father frowned. "Is that how you met Kacey?"

"No, I met her the old-fashioned way, through friends. A bunch of us went out for drinks after work and she joined us." His ex-wife was pretty, but what had attracted him was that she was so full of life. Kacey loved an adventure and wanted to try everything. They'd had so much fun, traveled on several vacations together, and he fell hard. He proposed after only nine months, and they married in Vegas a month later. Neither one of them wanted to wait.

"Hmmm. I always thought you should have waited before you married her. You need to spend four seasons with a person to really know them."

Travis nodded. He didn't disagree.

"So, this online dating thing. I hear it can be good. You

can take your time and make sure you find someone compatible before you even meet them."

Travis looked at his father closely. "Dad, are you ready to get back out there? If you are, I think online dating is a great idea."

"Not for me!" His father looked horrified at the thought. "It's only been five years since your mother passed. I can't imagine I could find someone like her again. It's you I'm thinking of."

"You think I should start online dating?" Travis was amused at the thought.

"I think it might be a good idea, yes. You and Sophie have been living with me for just over a year now and I love having you here, but I don't think you've gone on a single date in that time?"

"Well, I've been pretty busy, between finding a property for the house and getting started on the building, running my business remotely and raising Sophie by myself."

"Time goes by fast, too fast. It's nice to have someone to share your life with."

"I do have someone. I have Sophie," Travis said. But he knew what his father meant. He just hadn't been ready to go there yet, with anyone.

His father just shook his head. "Just an idea. There's no harm in giving it a try—at least see who is out there. Because you won't meet anyone hanging out with me and Sophie."

Travis laughed. "You may have a point there. I'll think about it."

"Good."

Later that night, after his father went to bed, Travis was

still wide awake, flipping channels and finding nothing of interest to watch. His mind drifted back to his father's suggestion, and he opened up his laptop.

The main dating site for the Cape and Islands seemed to be Perfect Match. His main hesitation was putting his picture up. Nantucket was a small island and Travis had grown up there. After college, he'd taken a job at a tech company in San Francisco and a few years later developed a software product and founded a company to sell it. For years he lived on ramen noodles, Red Bull and beer as all of his money and that of his angel investors went into growing his startup.

When they came back to Nantucket every summer for a few weeks, they always stayed with his father. When the startup took off, his name and picture were all over the internet. People knew he was back on Nantucket—he was always recognized when he went grocery shopping or stopped into one of the bars downtown. It was nice living somewhere where people had known him all his life, but it was a little much with the added notoriety to put his photo on a dating site. He decided to start without a photo—even though all the advice went against it.

But he didn't want people interested in dating him because they were curious about him and his company—or his bank account. Nantucket was an affluent community in some ways—but the majority of people that lived there year-round were more middle-class. He just didn't want anyone pre-judging him because of his photo.

He knew no photo also meant less interest, and he was okay with that. He started a profile and struggled over what to say. It was hard to sum up your personality in a snappy sentence or two. He decided to just be brutally honest rather than trying to sell himself.

"Recently divorced—just over a year, single father of a beautiful four-year-old daughter. My father strongly suggested that I do this. And his advice is usually worth taking, so here we are. Friends say I'm a laid-back type A. Pretty relaxed and chill but also driven and focused when it comes to work. But I'm all about balance. Used to be a workaholic, now I like to end my day at five or so and go to the beach with my daughter and sometimes my father. We like to fish, and I love surfing.

I also really like working with my hands, and am building a sleigh bed for my daughter. It's a nice change from my day job, which is mostly computer work. I'm not much of a cook, but I can grill just about anything. Always up for going to dinner or to hear some live music. Sorry about the no photo. For privacy reasons, am starting out this way. Let's chat first and go from there."

Before he could change his mind, Travis hit send and sighed. It would be interesting to see if anyone would reach out to him without a picture. He was suddenly exhausted and decided to head to bed. He'd check tomorrow and do a search of his own. It didn't seem fair to reach out to anyone that had their photos up if he didn't have his up, though. Maybe there would be someone interesting that didn't have any pictures either—that would be a good, slow start.

4

"*We* didn't get the Harrison project." Beth said as Chase walked into the office to have lunch with her. Beth had been the office manager at Chase's company before she and Chase started dating. She'd always loved working with him, even more so now that they were married.

Whenever work permitted, if the job site was nearby or he was able to take the time, Chase liked to eat lunch with his wife. And Beth appreciated the company. It was a nice break mid-day, as she was usually alone in the office while Chase and his employees were in the field.

Chase frowned at the news and stopped in front of her desk. Beth put the phones on voicemail and grabbed her sandwich and water, and they both went into the conference room and sat at the big oval table where they met with prospective clients. Once they were settled, Beth shared the details of the email she'd read just moments before Chase arrived.

"Tony said he was planning on using you, but money

is tight on this project and there was another bid that was significantly lower. He said he didn't really have a choice."

Chase unwrapped his turkey sandwich and glared at it before taking a bite. "Our bid was reasonable. I try to be as fair as possible. Did he say who he went with?"

"He did, but I wasn't familiar with the name. Maybe you know them? Cardoso Construction."

"Cardoso. Hmmmm. I have heard that name a few times recently. I think they're new. I don't know much more than that, though."

"Do you think they're lowballing just to win some bids?" Beth asked. They'd run into it a few times in the past, but not for a while. Fortunately, the market was still strong and there was plenty of work to go around.

"Could be. I don't know any Cardosos on Nantucket. Maybe they're new to the island and just getting started."

"On a different note, Travis stopped by this morning with his daughter, Sophie. She is so cute."

Chase smiled slightly. "She is a cute little thing. What were they up to?"

"I'd emailed Travis to let him know the new catalogs I was waiting on came in and I had a few ideas I wanted to run by him." While Chase handled the actual construction side of things, Beth had gotten more involved with the interior design and loved helping their clients bring their vision to life.

"Yeah? What did he think? Did you find the tile you were looking for?"

She nodded. "Yes. And he loved it. Hold on, I'll show you." Beth jumped up and went for the catalogs and put them on the conference table between them. She opened to the page she'd shown Travis.

"This one, the deep, smoky-gray subway tile. I thought it would look great with a creamy French vanilla cupboard. The tile gives a masculine feel and the cupboards some warmth." Beth thought it would look gorgeous. Travis and Sophie had agreed. Though Sophie was excited about everything. She'd had fun playing with a pile of tile samples while Beth and Travis chatted.

"That does look cool. This place is going to be great when we finish. Travis agreed to let us use pictures in our online portfolio, too. That will help us win bids for more high-end homes."

Travis' house was Beth's favorite so far that Chase had built. It wasn't a huge house, not like some of the mansions on the island. It was just over three thousand square feet, four bedrooms, and was a rustic contemporary design with lots of big windows and glass sliders that opened out onto a deck that overlooked Nantucket Sound. The house had soaring cathedral ceilings in the main living area, which was an open concept—the kitchen on one side, a big dining table in front of the window and beyond that the family room.

Travis had chosen wooden beams that ran the length of the room and gave a bit of a mountain feel. The lot was at the top of a hill and the views were spectacular.

"Travis wants to hold off on finishing the basement. He's anxious to get moved in. I suggested he live with it for a bit and then decide what he wants to do."

Chase nodded. "That's fine. We're just about done. He can get in there next week."

19

"He said he'll call us once he knows what he wants," Beth added.

"That works." Chase paced around the office, still frustrated. "I can't believe we didn't get that bid. I really thought Tony was going to go with us," Chase said.

"He was, but the bids were just so far apart. He said he'll definitely call you for a future project. He seemed sincere," Beth said.

"Oh I'm sure he will. Tony's a good client. I just wonder how the heck Cardoso is going to make any money."

5

"*A*re you sure you don't want to come into town and do a little shopping with me? There might be some good sales. They usually start this time of year." Victoria's mother stood in the kitchen doorway, her Kate Spade black and white tote bag slung over her shoulder. She was ready to go.

Victoria shook her head and took a sip of her coffee. She'd slept in and had a bit of a headache. Prosecco always seemed to do that to her, but she loved it anyway. And it had been a fun night out after work. After she and Taylor finished Victoria's online dating profile, they'd walked over to B-ACK Yard BBQ to meet the others for a few drinks and some food.

"No, I'm feeling lazy. I might try to do some writing. Let me know if there are any good sales."

"All right." Her mother looked at her curiously. "When are you going to let me read some of this story you're working on?"

Victoria laughed. "Maybe never. It's a long way from

being done and even longer from being in any condition for me to show anyone. I'm just having fun—it might not go anywhere."

"You're a good writer. I'm sure it's wonderful."

Victoria loved that her mother always seemed to be confident that whatever Victoria set her mind to, she could be successful. Victoria usually didn't have any issues with confidence, but writing fiction was a funny thing. She seemed to alternate between loving what she was writing and thinking it was the worst thing ever. She smiled at her mother in appreciation. "Thank you. Good luck with the shopping."

Her mother left and Victoria topped off her coffee, filling it to the brim before adding a generous spoonful of sugar. She'd tried to drink her coffee black a few times, but it just wasn't the same without the sugar.

She grabbed her laptop and headed out to the farmer's porch and her favorite spot, an oversized swing sofa. This time of morning, the sun was the strongest there, and she happily curled up on the soft cushions. She let the sun wash over her as she tapped her feet on the deck to push the swing and closed her eyes as it swayed back and forth.

This was her routine before she started writing new words. She needed a little time to sit and think about what she wanted to do for her first scene of the day. The fiction writing was all a big experiment—something she'd tried on a whim one day, soon after the breakup with Todd when she'd been feeling especially alone.

Even though she'd realized he wasn't the one, and the breakup was probably for the best, Victoria had felt a bit adrift as she'd had the rest of her life totally planned out.

The wedding details were almost finalized, and they'd been talking about building a house. That's why she hadn't minded moving home with her parents when she took the job at the newspaper, because she knew it was temporary.

She had mixed feelings now about living at home. Part of her was anxious to get her own place again—she'd loved having her own apartment when she lived in Boston. But the other part was glad for the company—it was nice to have both of her parents around. Her mother's fussing used to annoy her when she was younger, but now she appreciated the attention and the delicious, home-cooked meals. Cooking was not one of Victoria's strong points. It had never interested her, and pizza and takeout were just so easy. Her mother had volunteered to show her some basics, though, and Victoria realized it might not be a bad idea to take her up on it.

She opened her laptop and pulled up the story she'd been working on. She'd surprised herself by how much she was enjoying trying to write fiction. Working as a reporter was such a black and white thing, which Victoria appreciated and she'd always loved chasing a hot story. This was totally different. It had started as a way to fill the time and get her mind off being annoyingly single again after being part of a couple for so long. The last thing she felt like doing was 'getting back out there' and trying to date.

What had surprised her the most when she starting playing around with writing fiction was that of all the possible stories she could write—adventure, mystery, suspense, something literary—what she'd felt drawn to the most was romance. Romantic-comedy, to be specific. She'd always loved watching screwball romantic comedy movies, with their witty banter, and she also loved reading slightly steamy romance.

So, she decided to mash it all into her own kind of story and started writing just to amuse herself, with no regard to how well it would sell. Initially, she'd had no intentions of actually doing anything with it. But, now that she was three-quarters of the way into the story, she was starting to wonder if other people might possibly like it, too.

This particular scene was giving her a hard time, though. She wasn't exactly sure what needed to happen. Usually she could just start writing and it would come to her, but today the words weren't coming. And when she reread what she'd written, she was tempted to delete it all. She worried that it was boring and that was her biggest fear—she didn't want to bore the reader. Though she'd learned to just wait and read it again later. Almost always, it was better than she'd thought. But today she was pretty sure it just wasn't very good.

And all the banging from the house next door didn't help matters. It was hard to lose herself in the story when she kept getting distracted by the loud sounds of hammering and a chainsaw. Finally, she decided to take a break and walk around the yard a bit. Walking sometimes helped her focus on what needed to happen next when she wasn't sure what to write.

Victoria was on her third lap around the house before a good idea came to her and she was so lost in her thoughts that she almost didn't see the tall, tanned man leaning against the low wood fence that separated their lots. He was holding a hammer and wearing a short-sleeve t-shirt. It was a warmer day than usual for this time of year and he'd worked up a sweat. His muscled arms glistened in the sun.

He looked vaguely familiar to her, but she couldn't place him. She figured he must be one of Chase's workers. Though she was surprised to see anyone working on a Saturday. She didn't see Chase's truck in the driveway. Just an old jeep. Maybe the guy was putting in some overtime. She was glad the pounding had stopped. Maybe he was done now and she could write her next scene in peace and quiet.

He met her gaze and nodded. "Sorry for the noise. Just noticed you were sitting outside. Hope it wasn't too annoying. I'm just about done."

"It was annoying actually," The words came out a little more sharply than she'd intended and she immediately smiled to soften the effect. "Chase doesn't usually have workers out here on the weekends."

"I don't work for Chase. It's my place, actually. I'm just anxious to get moved in and wanted to get this swing set put together for my daughter. Like I said, though, I'm pretty much done."

Victoria looked over the fence and saw what he'd been working on. A huge wooden swing set sat in the backyard. It was gorgeous. Victoria would have loved it when she was a kid.

"How old is your daughter?" She'd never been all that into children, but felt bad that she'd snapped at him. He seemed nice enough, and he was done with the banging, after all.

"Sophie is four. You'll have to meet her when we move

in." He paused for a moment before shaking his head and saying, "You don't remember me, do you?"

She had no idea who he was. "I thought you looked familiar," she said.

"Well, I would hope so. You broke my heart in tenth grade." He grinned. "Travis Sturgess."

Her mouth fell open. "I'm so sorry. You look so different. High school was another lifetime ago." She'd dated Travis for a few weeks, before Todd asked her out, and that was it. Until he dumped her recently, of course. Travis was a boy then, thinner, shorter, nothing like the man that stood before her. And she knew he'd done well for himself. Something in the tech world. She'd heard the buzz that he was living back on Nantucket, but hadn't given it much thought.

"You look the same. Last I heard, you were still with Todd—and engaged. Congratulations."

Ugh. "We recently broke up, actually. He moved off-island."

A range of emotions flashed across Travis's face, surprise, followed by awkwardness and then sympathy. "I'm sorry. I didn't know. Breakups are tough."

"It's fine. We'd dated so long, I'm just taking some time to myself." She laughed. "One of my friends wants me to try online dating. I'm not sure I'm ready for that."

"Funny, my father was pushing for me to do that, too. I've done it in the past, and it's fine. I'm not sure I'm ready yet either. My divorce was final just a few months ago. Though we'd been separated for over a year."

"Oh, I'm sorry to hear that. Does your ex live on the

island too?" Victoria guessed that she probably did since they had a child together.

But Travis shook his head. "No. She's an actress and when she's not off on location filming, she lives in LA. Nantucket isn't exciting enough for her." She noticed a trace of bitterness in his voice.

"Does she see your daughter at all?" Though she'd never been the maternal type, Victoria couldn't imagine a mother abandoning her child totally.

"She was here for a month or so over the summer, in between shoots. She gets here when she can. It's not ideal, but it's better than nothing. She never wanted children."

"Oh. I see." But she didn't. Not really.

Travis sighed. "To her credit, she was always honest about that. I thought I didn't mind because I was so crazy about her. But then she accidentally got pregnant, and that's sort of where things fell apart for us. I wanted the baby, and she didn't. She agreed to have it, but said it would be my responsibility. And here we are."

Victoria glanced at the house, which was almost finished, and changed the subject. "Is this just a summer house, then? You run a business somewhere else?"

"This is going to be our year-round house. We've been staying with my father. I want Sophie to know him and to grow up in the same small town that I grew up in. It's a great place to live."

"It really is. I just moved back here a little over a year ago myself. I was working at a newspaper in Boston and something opened up here. It's funny, I wasn't excited about moving back here and did it because I was getting married. But now that the wedding is off, I'm not in any hurry to leave. I'd forgotten how much I love it here."

"Exactly. My company is based on the West Coast, but I just work remotely. It's all good." His phone buzzed, and he glanced down at it and smiled before answering. "Hi, honey. Yes, I'm almost done here. I think lunch at the Rose and Crown with Grampy sounds like a great idea." He hung up his phone and grinned. "I've been summoned. Nice catching up with you, Victoria. I'm sure I'll see you soon."

"You too, Travis. Nice seeing you."

She watched him walk away for a moment before heading back to her comfy spot on the swing sofa. Travis had really grown up. In high school, he'd been cute, but she'd quickly forgotten about him when Todd showed interest. Now he was handsome, and those muscled arms and flat stomach. Travis didn't look like he sat behind a desk. If it wasn't for his being a father, she might be tempted. But as attractive as he was, she couldn't imagine becoming a stepmother to a four-year-old. Though she'd figured that someday she would marry and have a child or two, it was never something she'd been eager to do. She'd never babysat or ever spent much time around small children. It was too bad. He checked off all her boxes otherwise.

6

Kay fell into bed after dinner and slept soundly. She woke later than usual the next morning, feeling refreshed and ready to start exploring. She'd left the curtains open a bit, and the sun streamed through the windows, promising a clear day. She eased herself out of bed and padded to the window to get a good look at the ocean. The waves were tipped with white and bigger than she remembered from her last visit. She knew that meant the wind was high. She'd need a warm coat for her beach walk.

Even though she'd slept in, it was still early. Kay usually woke between five and six, and it was just seven. She decided to take a quick shower before heading out to the beach and would go to breakfast at the inn when she returned.

A half hour later, wearing her favorite jeans, sneakers, fisherman knit sweater and a flannel lined warm coat, she made her way to the beach. She had her cell phone with her so she could take some pictures if the mood struck.

Kay thought she might have the beach all to herself since it was so early, but there were already a few others out walking. She watched a golden retriever run and dance along the edges of the surf, jumping back every time its paws touched the water.

It was late September, so both the air and water were starting to cool. Kay always loved this time of year in New England. There were still plenty of good-weather days, but the crowds were gone. And it varied so much—one day might be sunny and warm in the seventies and two days later, it could be chilly enough to turn the heat on. She was grateful that today was sunny and in the sixties, though when the wind gusted it felt cooler.

There was a lighthouse down the beach a half mile or so, and that seemed like a good distance to aim for. Kay set off, walking close to the water's edge, where the sand was a bit firmer. She got some good shots of the beach and the lighthouse as she drew closer to it. The air smelled so clean and fresh. She took a deep breath, then turned to head back. Her stomach was beginning to remind her that it was time for breakfast.

When she was almost back at the inn, she noticed a man with thick white hair and a bright red baseball cap. He looked to be about her age and he was holding a long metal device and sweeping it across the sand in front of him. He was very intent on what he was doing and didn't look up as Kay approached him.

"Is that a metal detector?" Kay had never seen one up close before, but knew that people sometimes liked to use them on the beach.

The man looked up and smiled when he saw her. His

eyes were big and brown and his smile was warm. "Yes, my son got this for me recently. I've only tried it out a few times. So far, no treasure has been found. But I keep hoping."

Kay laughed. "It looks like fun. I've never tried it before."

"You should give it a try. I'm Walter, by the way. Walter Sturgess. I live right over there." He pointed at a modest blue-gray Cape Cod-style house that was just a few doors down from The Beach Plum Cove Inn.

"I'm Kay, Kay Johnson. I'm staying at the inn. Lisa Hodges is an old family friend."

Walter nodded. "I've known Lisa since she moved here many years ago. She and Rhett are good people. Is this a quick visit, or will you be here a bit?"

Kay smiled. "I don't have an actual end date. I was planning for about two months or so. Maybe head down to Charleston after that."

"I hear it's a little warmer down there. Never been myself. Is that where you're from?"

"No. I'm from Arlington. I lived in the Boston area all my life. My husband passed two years ago, and I just thought I was ready to do a little traveling."

She saw the sympathy in Walter's eyes as he spoke. "I'm sorry for your loss. The first few years are tough. I lost my Margery five years ago. Still miss her every day. But, I've got my son and my granddaughter staying with me now. It's nice to have them around."

"I bet it is." Kay thought of her son so far away in Japan. "You're lucky to have them nearby. How old is your granddaughter?"

Walter's smile lit up his face. "Sophie is four, cute as a button and old for her age. She keeps me on my toes."

Kay's stomach growled loudly, and she almost died with embarrassment. She hoped that Walter hadn't heard. If he did, he didn't say anything.

"Well, it was nice chatting with you. I told Lisa I'd be down for breakfast, so I should be on my way."

"Of course. Say, why don't you give this a try?" He handed her the metal detector and it was tempting. Kay was curious to try it, but didn't want to take it from him.

"Oh, no that's okay."

"Go ahead. I'm all done for today. You can bring it back to me in a day or two. No hurry. I usually go for a walk most mornings, then have my coffee after. You can join me for a cup then if you have the time."

Kay took the metal detector. "Thank you. I'll try it out tomorrow and then bring it by after if that works?"

"Perfect. I'll be there."

Kay was still smiling as she walked into the house and brought the metal detector up to her room. She looked forward to trying it out the next morning. She headed to the dining room and there were several tables of people eating breakfast. Lisa and Rhett were sitting at a small round table and waved for her to join them. Kay poured herself a coffee and added a little milk. One of the breakfast options was a red pepper quiche, but she decided on a delicious-looking ramekin of overnight oats, topped with raspberries in a little syrup, toasted coconut and slivered almonds. She added a few slices of cantaloupe on the side and made her way to Lisa's table.

"Did you go for your beach walk?" Lisa asked as Kay sat down.

"I did. It was a gorgeous morning for it. And I met one of your neighbors. Walter Sturgess."

Lisa smiled. "Walter's a nice guy. I felt so bad for him when he lost his wife a few years ago. She was a sweetheart. I think he's doing better now, though. Especially since he has his son and granddaughter staying with him."

Kay nodded as she took a bite of cantaloupe. "He mentioned that. I'm sure they are good company for him. He was using his metal detector and insisted I take it and try it out next time I walk on the beach."

"Oh, that sounds like fun. I've never done that either. I'm glad you met him."

"I am too."

"So, what's on your agenda today?" Lisa asked.

"I thought I might head into town and explore a bit. Maybe find that needlepoint shop you mentioned."

"Oh, you can't miss it. It's right on India Street. Don't forget about dinner tonight—all the kids are coming. We will have a full house."

"I look forward to it. Can I help you do anything?"

Lisa thought for a moment. "I think I'm all set. I told everyone to be here around six. Just come then and have a good time."

Rhett took the last sip of his coffee and stood. "On that note, I'm off to the restaurant to do the weekly ordering. I will see you ladies later today."

After Rhett left, Lisa told Kay about the menu for dinner as she finished her breakfast.

"I'm making a big pot of seafood chowder. I'll be heading downtown myself in a bit, to stop at Trattel's Seafood and get everything I need. After that, we're having prime rib, popovers, baked potatoes and roasted Brussels sprouts."

"That sounds so good. I'll make sure to eat a light lunch."

Lisa laughed. "That's probably a good idea. If you are still downtown around lunchtime, you might pop into The Corner Table. They always have good soups and salads."

"Perfect." Kay took her last bite of oatmeal and polished off her coffee. "All right, I think it's time for me to get moving. Breakfast was delicious. Thank you."

Lisa looked pleased by the compliment. "It was my pleasure. Have fun exploring."

7

*K*ay put the address of the needlepoint shop in the car's GPS and set off for downtown Nantucket. She was pretty sure she knew the way, but she liked the security of the GPS advising her, as she'd only made the drive downtown once, when she'd followed Rhett to the inn.

Fifteen minutes later, she turned onto Main Street and then onto India. She passed by the needlepoint shop as she looked for a parking spot and found one a few doors down. She'd already signed up for the class, but wanted to stop in and say hello to the store owner and browse the store a bit.

Kay stepped into the shop and took a look around. There was a warm, welcoming feel to the room and a lovely smell that she couldn't quite place-it was a mix of cinnamon, cloves and maybe apple? There were a few big candles around the room that were glowing cheerfully and as she drew closer, the scent grew stronger. There were several people browsing the different needlepoint kits, yarns, and supplies. Kay slowly strolled around the store, looking everything over while soft jazz music played in the background.

"Is there anything in particular that you're looking for?" A friendly voice asked. Kay turned and saw a petite woman with wavy gray hair and a cheerful smile. She looked to be a little younger than Kay.

"I actually signed up online for the needlepoint class that starts next Tuesday. I thought I might get a head start and pick up some supplies. Any suggestions?"

"Oh, how marvelous. I'll be teaching the class. I'm Connie. What is your name?"

Kay told her. "Oh, you're the one that is going to be staying here for a few months, if I remember, right?"

Kay nodded. "That's right." She'd mentioned it in her note when she signed up for the class.

"You picked a lovely time to visit the island. The weather is still nice, but the crowds are gone. Now, let's think about this for a minute. You'll get some supplies in your class kit. I can give you that now if you like and maybe you might want to pick up some additional thread and perhaps an easy beginner's project to play with?"

"That sounds perfect. I thought it might be a nice way to pass an afternoon or evening."

"Oh, it is! It's very relaxing. I think you will enjoy it." Connie led her over to a wall full of various projects. "This is a good one. We'll be making ornaments in the class, so how about coasters? They are easy and practical. You'll be able to use them anytime."

Connie handed her the package and Kay loved the

bright, beachy look of the coasters. The design had a sailboat and lighthouse on the beach.

"I love it."

Connie led Kay to the register and retrieved her class bag of materials from the back of the shop.

"Okay, you're all set." Connie handed Kay back her credit card and a shopping bag with her purchases. "See you next Tuesday!"

Kay was still smiling as she walked outside and stashed her bag in her car. She spent the next few hours roaming around downtown, popping in and out of different shops until it was lunchtime. She decided to take Lisa's advice and get some soup or a salad at The Corner Table.

When she stepped inside, the scent of curry and garlic teased her senses. The soup of the day was a curried chicken vegetable. Kay ordered a cup of the soup and a slice of their citrus olive oil cake for dessert. She took a seat by the window and people-watched as she ate her lunch. As she was finishing up, she heard a familiar voice and looked up to see Walter Sturgess and a young girl that she assumed was his granddaughter, Sophie.

Walter stopped short when he saw her. "Well, look at that. Fancy running into you again." He looked at his granddaughter and smiled. "Sophie, this is Kay, the lady I told you about. She's going to try her luck with the metal detector soon."

"It's nice to meet you, Sophie."

Sophie looked at her with interest. "Grampy hasn't found anything yet with that metal detector."

Kay laughed. "I probably won't either."

"You never know. You might have the magic touch." He glanced at Kay's empty dishes. "How was your lunch?"

"It was excellent. I just wanted something light as Lisa's having a big dinner tonight. Are the two of you having lunch?"

Sophie shook her head vigorously. "We're here for the mud cake."

"We already ate at home, but I had to run some errands and Sophie said she'd join me as long as we could come here for some mud cake. So we're going to split a piece."

"It's a very big piece," Sophie explained.

Kay stood. "Well, that sounds delicious. Don't let me keep you."

Walter nodded. "Enjoy the rest of your day. I'll see you soon, I hope?"

Kay smiled. "I'll stop by tomorrow. After I try out the metal detector."

"Good luck!" Sophie said, then ran to the counter to order her cake.

"I'll see you tomorrow." Walter said with a smile before turning to join his granddaughter.

8

*L*isa was pleased with her first attempt at making popovers. They were so simple to make, just flour, butter, salt, eggs and milk. She and Rhett had them recently at Boston Chops, a steakhouse in the South End of Boston. They'd gone for a weekend getaway and stayed in the Back Bay. They went to the Museum of Fine Arts, saw a new musical that was on its way to Broadway after opening in Boston and a highlight of the trip had been that dinner and the light and fluffy popovers that had melted in her mouth. She'd been craving them ever since.

As she took the second batch of popovers out of the oven, the front door opened and her daughter Kate, husband, Jack and their twins arrived. Her son Chase and wife Beth were right behind them, followed a few minutes later by Abby, her husband Jeff, and their daughter, Natalie. Kay was the next to arrive and looked a bit nervous as she stepped into the crowded family room. Lisa saw her and waved her into the kitchen. Kay handed her a bottle of cabernet.

"Peter at Bradford Liquors said this is one of your favorites."

Lisa's eyes widened when she saw the label. It was Charles Krug and one Lisa loved to splurge on for special occasions.

"Thank you. You shouldn't have."

Kay laughed. "I like a good wine, too."

"Thank you, Kay," Rhett said. He reached for the bottle. "I'll open this now and let it breathe a bit."

"We have a bottle of Josh open if you want to start with a glass of that?" Lisa offered.

Kay thought that was a great idea, and as Lisa was pouring her a glass of wine, Kristen and Tyler arrived. They were always the last ones to arrive at any gathering, but they weren't too late.

Lisa set out a bowl of spiced nuts and an assortment of cheeses and crackers. Everyone snacked and chatted until it was time to head into the dining room. They had the seafood chowder first. Her kids loved it and she hadn't made it in ages. It had shrimp, scallops, cod and lobster in a buttery cream base with a hint of sherry.

"Lisa, this is amazing. I'm savoring every spoonful," Kay raved. Lisa was pleased to hear it and thanked her.

When they were done, she put the popovers back in the oven for a quick minute to warm them up.

Rhett carried the big tray of carved prime rib to the long dining table and set it in the center. Lisa and the girls brought everything else over, a sour cream and horse-radish sauce, au jus, the popovers, baked potatoes, and Brussels sprouts.

Everyone gathered around the table. Kate and Abby had

fed the children earlier, and they were content in the living room watching TV. Rhett noticed Kay's wineglass was empty, and jumped up and returned a moment later with the bottle of wine she'd brought.

"I think this has had enough time to breathe." He filled Kay's glass and set the bottle on the table so people could help themselves when they were ready.

He raised his glass. "I'd like to say a toast to thank everyone for coming today. It's been too long since we've had everyone together for Sunday dinner. And we're glad that Kay is with us today."

Everyone raised their glasses in agreement before diving in.

Conversation was lively around the table as they ate. Lisa had talked to her children throughout the week, but there was so much going on in their lives that there was always news.

"I have some really exciting news," Kate said, with a gleam in her eye.

Everyone looked her way. Kate had been busy getting her kids fed and settled, so she hadn't had a chance to fill anyone in yet. Lisa had just talked to her daughter a few days ago, and was very curious what had happened since then that had her so excited.

"So, they are almost ready to start shooting for the TV series. I got a call this morning with an update." She paused dramatically.

"They called you on a Sunday? That's wonderful, honey," Lisa said.

"Yes, they called because there's now a major star attached. Cami Carmichael read the book and her production company reached out to my agent to see if they could option it."

"But it's already optioned, right?" Lisa wasn't sure how it all worked.

Kate nodded. "Yes, and they are working on a limited series for Netflix. But they had only just started on the casting, so they put her in touch with the producers that have the option and they struck a deal. Cami is going to star in it—and it's going to be filmed here."

"It's going to be filmed on Nantucket?" Kristen asked.

"Yes. Cami is based here now, and the story is set on Nantucket, so the producers are going to make it happen. Which means I'll get to visit the set, too."

"Oh, honey, I'm so excited for you. Do you know when they will start filming?"

"Soon. They're going to work with her availability and she has a break in her schedule for the next six months. So, they are going full-speed on casting and getting everything else that they need."

"Congratulations Kate," Kay said. "I actually picked up a copy of that book at Mitchell's bookstore earlier today when I was shopping downtown. I'm looking forward to reading it."

Everyone chimed in to offer their congratulations. Lisa was excited for Kate. Cami was a famous movie actress that came to Nantucket on vacation and ended up falling in love with the chef at The Whitley Hotel, where she stayed for several months. They were engaged now, and she considered Nantucket home. Lisa knew that she'd met her daughters through their friend Mia, who worked as a wedding planner and had also stayed at the inn for a while when her condo was being renovated.

"She goes by a different name, doesn't she?" Lisa couldn't remember it.

"Yes, her real name is Bella. We all met her through Mia at one of her girls' nights. She asked me about my books, but I really didn't expect that she'd read one." Kate still seemed dazed by it all.

"She has good taste." Rhett grinned. "I felt badly for her that time the media got wind that she and Nick were at the restaurant."

Lisa remembered that. Rhett had told her about it on the ride home that night. She'd had to pick him up because he'd slipped his car keys to Bella's boyfriend, Nick, so they could go out the back exit and drive Rhett's truck back to the hotel.

"I can't imagine living like that. With people following you around," Lisa said.

Kate laughed. "I can't either. Fortunately, it doesn't happen to writers."

Lisa glanced across the table at her quietest daughter, Kristen, who was picking at her potato. She was always her fussy eater, and had stopped eating meat recently, so Lisa had also made her a bowl of steamed veggies.

"Kristen, how are you liking the new studio? Are you all settled in?" When Kristen and Tyler married over the summer, she moved into his cottage next door and Chase started on renovations to Tyler's cottage, building an adjacent studio so Kristen could do her painting there.

"Yes, and it's perfect. As you know, I was reluctant to give up my sun-filled studio, but the one that Chase built for me is even bigger and brighter. The sunlight just pours in."

"That's great, honey. I can't wait to see it soon."

Kristen smiled. "I'll have you over this week, maybe coffee Monday or Tuesday. I just wanted to wait until it was all set up."

"Either day works for me. Will you put the cottage on the market soon, do you think?"

Kristen and Tyler exchanged glances. "I think we might hang onto it and see if there's rental interest. I was thinking short term, summers and maybe weekends off-season. I'd love to pick your brain about that, actually."

"Oh, that's a great idea. Your location is so close to everything. I bet there will be plenty of demand for it," Lisa said. Their cottages were near downtown and a short walk to the beach. Tyler actually had the cottage next to Kristen's, and that's how they'd met. He was also a successful author of suspense novels, and both he and Kristen worked from home. Lisa thought they were well-suited, and she didn't want to ask, but she hoped they might want to start a family soon.

So far, two of her daughters had children. She wondered about Chase and Beth too, if they might be ready soon. Not that Lisa was in a rush, but she did love seeing her grandchildren. Kate had the twins and Abby had one girl so far, and was pregnant with her second.

"Chase, I drove by one of your houses the other day, the big one on the ocean. It looks almost done. Gorgeous home. Is that the one for that famous tech guy?" Jeff asked.

Chase nodded. "Yeah, it's Travis Sturgess's house. And it's very close to being done. It's coming along fast now."

"Who is Travis?" Kate asked. "The name sounds familiar. I feel like I should know who he is."

"He started a tech company that took off. His technology is used in almost every office now," Chase said.

"Is that a summer house, then?" Rhett asked.

"No. He's from Nantucket. We were in the same homeroom class. Travis is a good guy. He has full custody of his daughter and wants to raise her here. They're staying with his father for now."

"And Walter is loving it," Lisa said. "I think that saved him after he lost Margery. They've been with him for over a year now."

"Walter is such a sweet man," Kate said. "He and Margery always had lollipops for us if we wandered over his way."

"He did," Kristen confirmed. "And Margery made the best fudge. I'm sure it's been hard for him."

"He seems like a lovely man," Kay agreed, and explained how she'd met him on the beach.

"That's nice that he lent you his metal detector," Kate said. "Maybe you'll strike it rich and find something exciting."

Kay laughed. "I'm not expecting anything like that. Walter said he hasn't found a thing yet. But I am looking forward to trying it."

Once everyone finished eating and the table was cleared, Lisa set out coffee, a tray of Italian cookies and a plate of brownies that Kristen had baked and brought over. Everyone protested that they were full, but Lisa wasn't surprised when most of them helped themselves to either a cookie or a brownie.

"Mom, how are the online sales going?" Kate asked. Lisa had an ecommerce site where she sold some of the dishes that were popular with her guests, like her lobster quiche. Business had been so good that she'd outgrown her kitchen and had a company making the quiches and other items for her now and shipping them out.

"They're not growing like they used to. There have been some up and down days lately and I'm not sure what to think of it. I have noticed a few other companies are making lobster quiche now too and selling it for a lower price than we are."

Kate frowned. "Did you ask Marley about it?" Lisa's friend Marley was a marketing consultant and had helped Lisa to set up the ecommerce site.

"I did. She wasn't worried about it and said she'd expected that might happen. She reminded me that mine was the first and the best, and customers will realize that."

"I agree with her," Rhett said. "If those others are so much cheaper, the quality isn't likely to be as good. It's probably nothing but claw meat in their quiches."

Lisa relaxed a little. She knew her quiches were good. But still, she was going to keep a close eye on daily sales and what those other sellers were doing.

---

9

*K*ay woke at her usual early hour. She'd gone to bed early the night before, full from Lisa's big roast beef dinner. It had been nice to see the whole family and catch up with them all.

It was still early, so she made herself a cup of coffee. There was a Keurig machine in the room and a small refrigerator and microwave, which was perfect. She'd stopped at the local grocery store the day before on her way home and picked up a few things, some soups and cold cuts for sandwiches, so she wouldn't have to eat out too often.

She sipped her coffee and read the news online for a bit before jumping in the shower and getting dressed. Since she was going to stop by Walter's after she tried out the metal detector, she decided to head to breakfast first, when it opened at eight.

The room was empty but the door to the dining room was open and all the food was set out, so Kay wandered over to take a look. The hot offering was scrambled eggs with what looked like pesto and slices of ham. She helped herself to some, along with a few home fries and a piece of rye toast with butter. As she was walking to a table with a fresh coffee and her breakfast, Lisa and Rhett arrived.

Rhett went straight to the coffee, poured himself a cup, and joined Kay at the table. A moment later, Lisa sat down with a plate of eggs and coffee.

Lisa's eyes twinkled as she asked, "How do you like the green eggs and ham?"

Kay laughed. "It's delicious, actually. I've never thought to add pesto to eggs before."

"Rhett taught me that. It was a new thing for me, too."

Kay glanced at Rhett who wasn't eating. "You're not hungry?"

Rhett smiled. "Oh, I'll have my share. I like to enjoy a cup of coffee first."

"Are you heading out to try your luck on the beach this morning?" Lisa asked.

Kay smiled. "Yes. I told Walter I'd stop by after and return the metal detector."

"He'll be glad for the company. I ran into him yesterday at Stop and Shop and he told me his son's house is almost done. They'll be moving out soon. Though Nantucket is so small, I'm sure he'll still see them often."

"Much better than being on the other side of the country," Rhett added.

"Did you stop at the needlepoint shop yesterday?" Lisa asked.

"I did. I was planning on playing around with it last night after dinner, but your food was so good. By the time I got back to my room I was too full and tired. I'm looking forward to the first class tomorrow night."

Lisa looked at her thoughtfully for a moment. "Kay, have you given any thought to dating at some point? Walter is right around your age."

Kay dropped her spoon. The thought hadn't crossed her mind.

"No, no thought at all. I can't imagine wanting to do that. I was very lucky to have had a wonderful life with Al. I'm sure Walter feels the same. I think he still misses his wife."

Lisa smiled. "It was just a thought. I think he'll be a good friend for you, at least."

After breakfast, Kay made her way down to the beach and as soon as she reached the sand, she turned the metal detector on and slowly waved it back and forth as she walked along. She got all excited when it finally beeped until she bent over to see what set it off and it was an aluminum tab from a can. She covered as much of the beach as she could as she walked towards Walter's house. The detector didn't beep again until she was almost ready to call it quits.

She bent over and saw the edge of something black sticking out of the sand. She reached over and gave it a tug and then gasped when she saw that it was a beautiful Movado ladies watch. It was all black with a pearl face. She knew that it wasn't an inexpensive watch and wondered if someone that had stayed at the inn might have lost it, or possibly someone that Walter knew, as it wasn't far from the stairs to his house.

She climbed the steps and knocked softly on his front

door. He opened it a moment later and looked pleased to see her.

"Come on in."

She stepped inside and handed him the metal detector. "So, how'd you do? Did you find any treasure?" He asked.

Kay grinned and held up the watch. "I found this not far from your steps. Do you know who it might belong to?"

Walter leaned over to take a closer look, and whistled softly. "Well, that's really something. It didn't come from this house. You got lucky!"

Kay laughed. "I think I did, but I feel badly that someone lost this. I'll ask Lisa if anyone reported a missing watch."

"That's a good idea. But, if not, it's finders, keepers. Enjoy it! Now, how about some coffee?"

Walter poured coffee for both of them and they sat in his sunroom, which faced the ocean. It was a comfortable, cheery room. Kay imagined that he and his wife must have spent a lot of time there, enjoying the view.

Kay discovered that Walter was easy to talk to. They chatted for over an hour and the time flew by. She learned that he'd worked for the post office as a letter carrier and had enjoyed it.

"It's a social job. You get to know everyone and it's a tight community here. It was nice to retire too, though. Margery and I did some traveling. We went to all the places we dreamed of seeing and did a few cruises. Do you like cruises?"

"I do. Al and I did some traveling, too. Our last trip was a riverboat cruise along the Mississippi. We enjoyed that."

"Have you done an Alaska cruise? That was going to be our next trip."

"No. I've heard it's wonderful, though."

The front door opened and Kay heard voices and a rush of running footsteps as a small child raced into the room and stopped short when she saw Kay.

Walter laughed. "You remember my granddaughter, Sophie." Sophie was followed by a tall, thirty-something year old man that Kay guessed was her father. "And my son, Travis. Kay is staying with Lisa and Rhett."

"Nice to meet you," Travis said. "I have to jump on a conference call in a few minutes. Do you mind keeping an eye on Sophie?"

"Of course not."

"Grampy, can I do your hair?" Sophie ran over and stood beside Walter and waited expectantly. He laughed and reached into his pocket and pulled out a comb.

"Here you go, young lady. Make it look good." He winked at Kay, and she understood this was a game they played often. Sophie took the comb and pushed an ottoman behind Walter's chair and stepped up on it so she could easily reach the back of his head. She started combing his hair carefully, over and over. It was very sweet and Kay could tell Walter loved it as much as Sophie did. When she finished, he opened his wallet and handed her a dollar bill. "Thank you very much! You're an excellent hair-dresser."

"Thanks, Grampy! Can I have some goldfish?"

"Help yourself, honey. You know where they are." Sophie ran off to the kitchen and Walter turned his attention back to Kay. They chatted for a few more minutes, but as much as she'd enjoyed visiting, she didn't want to take up too much of his time.

"I should probably get going. Thank you for the coffee and for letting me use the metal detector."

"Anytime." They both stood and Walter walked her to the door. As she was about to leave, he asked, "Say, do you like Scrabble?"

"Of course." She smiled. "Doesn't everyone?"

"Thursday night is Scrabble night here. We could use a fourth player if you care to join us? We usually do pizza too."

"I'd love to."

"Great, why don't you come on by around six?"

"I'll see you then."

Kay smiled as she walked along the beach on her way back to the inn. Walter felt like an old friend already and she looked forward to Scrabble night.

10

"So, any good responses? Have you set up any dates yet?" Taylor asked as soon as Victoria walked into the newsroom on Monday morning.

Victoria sat at her desk, which was right in front of Taylor's, and spun her chair around.

"I've gotten a few responses. But I wouldn't call any of them 'good.' Most of them just asked me to send a picture. Without making much of an effort to say anything more. So they were an instant delete. And then there was the guy who is almost sixty. He was also an instant delete. So, no dates yet."

Taylor laughed. "You know, if you would put up a few pictures, you'd get a ton of responses."

Victoria made a face. "I am so not ready for that." She turned her chair around, turned on her computer, and got to work. The morning flew by and around eleven-thirty she'd just started thinking about what to have for lunch when she got a notification for another response from Perfect Match. Curious, she clicked on it and expected to instantly delete, but it was actually the first interesting response she'd received. And he didn't have any pictures posted.

"I'm intrigued that you don't have a picture up, either. I'm slowly dipping my toes back into the dating waters. I am recently divorced and a single father of a four-year-old daughter. I grew up here and don't want everyone to know my business just yet. So that's my reason for no photos. Anyway, just wanted to say hello. If any of this intrigues you, drop me a note back."

Victoria immediately recalled her conversation with Travis. And that his father pushed him into trying online dating. It would make sense that he might be hesitant to post pictures. She debated whether to reply. She definitely wasn't interested in someone that already had children. But if it was Travis, she felt badly not replying at all, as she knew he was as hesitant as she was about online dating. So, she decided to just reply briefly.

"I understand. I grew up here too and Nantucket is a small place. I wanted to go slowly too. I'm still not sure I'm ready to do this, to be honest."

She clicked send and felt satisfied that she'd sent a reply and that would probably be the end of it.

"Did you bring lunch? I was thinking of walking over to The Corner Table and grabbing a salad if you want to join me?" Taylor asked.

"Sure. I'm ready to go anytime. Oh, and I finally got a decent response."

"What? Tell me everything."

Victoria laughed. "I'm not interested, but he seems like a nice guy. Just not right for me. I replied back to him, though."

Taylor looked confused. "I don't understand. Why isn't he right for you? And why did you write back to him? You could have just deleted him."

"Well, he's a single father. And I'm not ready to be a stepmother. That's not me."

"Okay, so again, why reply?"

"Well, I think maybe I know him." Victoria told her about seeing Travis and how he was reluctantly trying out online dating, too. "So, I didn't want to be rude and make him think I wasn't interested."

"But you're not."

"Well, yes, I know. But I just thought it seemed kinder to reply and be kind of wishy-washy so he won't want to take it further."

Taylor laughed. "Okay. Well, I'm starving, so let's go."

When Victoria returned from lunch and settled back at her desk, she was surprised to see a response to her message already. She clicked it open,

"I understand that. I'm not in any hurry either. So, how's your day going? I'm working remotely and am stuck in an update meeting with too many people and am bored silly. I'm still listening, of course, but am now multi-tasking by writing to you. So, what do you like to do for fun? A perfect day for me is plenty of sunshine and either out on the boat fishing or attempting to surf. I'm a better fisherman than a surfer."

Victoria made herself a cup of coffee and debated whether to reply back. She took a sip and then started typing.

"I love the beach, though I don't love fishing. I'm happy to eat anything people catch, though. I've never tried surfing."

A few minutes later, a reply came back. "You should try it sometime. Nothing else like it. Ok, heading into back-to-back meetings that I have to actually pay attention to. Enjoy the rest of your day."

Victoria smiled. It didn't seem like a response was needed to that, so maybe if she didn't write back, that would be the end of it.

11

*K*ay arrived at the needlepoint shop five minutes early for her first class. Half of the class had already arrived and were taking their seats around a big round table in a side room. Connie welcomed her when she stepped inside with a big smile.

"Go on in and find yourself a seat. We'll be starting shortly."

Kay did as instructed and took an empty seat next to a woman who looked to be about her age. A few others arrived a moment later and settled at the table. So far, they were all women, but Kay was a little surprised at the wide age range. There were several young women in their late twenties or maybe early thirties. A few others looked to be in their forties or maybe fifties. And the rest were close to Kay's age and older. It did not surprise her that it was all women.

The woman next to her caught Kay's eye and smiled. "Hi there. I'm Ginny."

"Kay. Have you lived here long? I'm just visiting for a few months."

"Close to forty years now. We came for our honeymoon and loved it so much we decided to move here." Ginny smiled but then a cloud passed over her eyes. "I lost my Jim a few years ago. We had a wonderful life together but I still miss him."

Kay nodded. "I'm sorry. My husband passed a few years ago too. I only just recently felt ready to do a little traveling. Nantucket is my first stop."

"How fun! Where are you off to next?"

"Charleston, I think. I went there once years ago and have always wanted to go back."

"I've never been there, but I've heard it's lovely."

"Okay ladies. We're ready to begin!" Connie took her seat at the head of the table and for the next two hours she explained the basics of needlepoint and they practiced a bit before starting on their first project, a Christmas ornament shaped like a candy cane.

Everyone introduced themselves and it was interesting listening to everyone's stories. Most of them were year-round on the island except for Kay and one other woman who was visiting with her children for a few months. They were mothers, grandmothers and young single women. All looking for something fun and creative to do. Kay and Ginny chatted here and there as they worked on their projects and Kay learned that Ginny also volunteered with the local food pantry.

"My friend's daughter Abby volunteers there too. Lisa was going to have her get in touch with me. I'm interested in helping out while I'm here if there's a need for it."

"Oh there definitely is. We can always use more volunteers to work a shift or help unload the truck and put food away when the deliveries arrive at the end of the month."

"I'll do anything."

"I'm working a shift Saturday morning. If you'd like to meet me there, I can show you the ropes and you can help us fill client orders?"

"I can do that." Kay laughed. "My schedule is pretty much wide open."

Ginny smiled. "Good, when Abby reaches out, just let her know I'm going to train you."

"Will do."

The evening flew by and Kay thoroughly enjoyed herself. Needlepoint wasn't hard, and she was almost finished with her first project when the class ended. She just had to put the final touches on her candy cane. And she thought she could do that at home. It had been fun chatting with all the women, especially Ginny. She was easy to talk to and Kay looked forward to the next session and seeing her at the food pantry on Saturday.

"*D*o you want to come with me to see Kristen's new studio?" Lisa asked Rhett.

They were sitting in the dining room for breakfast and were the only ones left. All the guests had already come and gone. Lisa sipped her coffee and kept Rhett company while he finished his eggs.

"No, I'm heading into the restaurant. We're getting a big delivery today and I want to oversee that. I may need to handle hosting duties, as Elise might not make it in today. She was looking under the weather yesterday, so I told her to stay home and rest up if she didn't feel better."

Lisa nodded. "Poor Elise. It doesn't usually get too crazy though at lunch this time of year?" Fall was Lisa's favorite time of year. While she appreciated the business the tourists brought and both her and Rhett's business benefited from it, she also enjoyed the calm that fell over the island once the mad rush of tourists died down.

"Well, I hope it's busy, but you're right, it won't be anything we can't handle." Rhett's watch dinged, and he glanced down at the message scrolling across the small screen. Lisa had given him an Apple Watch for Christmas and he didn't wear it for the longest time, but once he did, he was surprised by how much he liked getting email and text notifications on his watch. He looked up and smiled.

"I just got a reminder email about an event at The Whitley that we're invited to. It's wine tasting with appetizers. Might be fun."

"That sounds interesting. When is it?"

"In a few weeks, on a Monday night. Sounds like they are inviting some local businesses to build their referral network."

Lisa smiled. "Well, that would explain why my business didn't get an invitation. I'm happy to go with you, though."

When they were done, Lisa kissed Rhett goodbye, then cleared the dining room and put everything away. She grabbed a few leftover blueberry muffins and put them in a bag to bring to Kristen's house and planned to have one herself, as she'd only had coffee.

Kristen used to live in an adorable cottage near downtown and now she lived in an almost identical cottage a few steps away. She and Tyler, her husband, had met when he moved in next door. Lisa had some concerns at first when it looked like Kristen was getting serious with Tyler as he had a history of alcohol abuse and relapsed not long after his mother died. He went off-island to a rehab program and since then, he seemed to have it under control. Lisa liked Tyler. More importantly, he made Kristen happy, and that's all Lisa wanted for her children.

They were both home when she arrived. Tyler was in the kitchen pouring himself a cup of coffee and said a quick hello before heading back into his office, or as he called it, his 'writing cave'.

Kristen gave her a hug and squealed when she peeked in the paper bag that held the muffins.

"You made my favorite—blueberry."

Lisa smiled. "They're my favorite too, and I'm hungry. We can have them with our coffee after you show me your new studio."

"Right this way." Kristen led her through the living room and down a small hall to a door that opened into a spacious room with gleaming hardwood floors and a vaulted ceiling. There were enormous windows and a sliding glass door along one wall that let in a ton of light. The door opened onto a small stone patio that was surrounded by newly planted trees and bushes.

"We planted all kinds of perennials, so next spring the flowers will be breathtaking. Lots of tulips to start and knockout roses," Kristen said.

Lisa looked around and took it all in. Her son was a talented builder.

"It's really beautiful, honey. Chase did a great job."

She noticed Kristen already had all of her paints and canvases set up in the room and in the corner, there was a nearly-finished painting on the easel. Lisa walked over for a closer look and admired her daughter's work. She recognized the beach in the painting and the lighthouse. It was a lovely interpretation of the inn and the ocean at sunset, with a vibrant pink-purple sky and a dreamy, hazy mist over the water.

"Kristen, this is gorgeous."

"Thank you. It's not finished, but I think it's turning out okay."

Her daughter was always very quiet and humble, and sometimes even somewhat insecure about her art.

"It's beautiful honey. Is this a commissioned piece or just something you wanted to do?"

"Marley commissioned it, actually. She said the view of the sunset on our beach was one of the things she loved most about staying at the inn."

Lisa smiled. Marley had become a good friend. She'd stayed at the inn after getting divorced and was ready for a change after working with her husband on the West Coast in a wildly popular retail ecommerce company. Like many who visited the island, Marley fell in love with Nantucket and the lifestyle here and decided to stay.

"I can picture that in her living room, maybe over the fireplace. Or in her office." Marley had bought a beautiful waterfront home and now worked from her home office as a marketing consultant.

"She didn't mention which room she had in mind for it," Kristen said. "Are you ready for coffee? I want to get your advice about possibly listing my house with Airbnb."

They went back to the kitchen and Kristen poured coffee for both of them and put two muffins on paper plates. They sat at the kitchen table and chatted for almost an hour and Lisa had plenty of ideas to share with Kristen. She'd learned what worked well by trial and error when she first opened the inn, and Kristen asked lots of good questions. Lisa didn't want to overstay her welcome, though. She knew Kristen needed to get back to her painting. And Lisa had things to do too.

She was having a few of her friends over for dinner, and Kay too, but Marley was coming a bit earlier as she wanted to go over Lisa's reports for the past month, so Lisa had to gather that information this afternoon. Sales were definitely down some. Every morning, she checked the income report from the day before and it was good but there seemed to be a slight decline.

Kristen didn't seem to be in any hurry to get back to her painting, though. After they finished chatting about Airbnb, she had a new question for Lisa.

"How's the online business going for you? Are you still having fun with it?"

"Most of the time. As I mentioned on Sunday, though, there are a few competitors that have popped up selling similar lobster quiches. Marley's not worried. She's coming over later to go over some things with me. I can't help but be a little nervous about it, though. It hasn't been that long since we started using the outside company to make the quiches."

"I agree with Marley. I don't think you have to worry yet. It's normal for other people to see what you are doing and decide to try it too. But you were there first. And no one's quiches could possibly be better than yours!"

Lisa laughed. "I love you for saying that. I hope you're right."

"I am. On a different note, I have something else to ask you." She paused for a moment and took a sip of her coffee. Lisa wondered what was on her mind. Kristen was always her quiet one. She kept a lot of things to herself until they bubbled up and she had to say something.

"Did you always know you wanted to have kids?"

"Oh. Well, yes." Lisa thought for a moment. "I think it was more that it was just expected. I always just assumed we would once your father and I married. It's what people did. Once I found out that I was pregnant with twins, I alternated between being terrified and excited."

Kristen shuddered. "I honestly don't think I could handle twins. It just seems like... a lot. Kate's doing great though."

"She is. I have no doubt, though, that you'd handle it just as well. You rise to the occasion and do what you have to do."

"What if I'm not sure I want to have kids at all? Would that be weird?" Kristen bit her lower lip and Lisa could sense that she was really struggling with this.

"It's fine if you don't want to have kids. Have you and Tyler talked about this? What does he want?"

"We have. It's not that I don't want to have them. It's just that I've never dreamed about having them. I've never felt that urge that a lot of my friends feel. I think I'd be perfectly content with it just being me and Tyler." She took a sip of her coffee and stared out the window. "He says he's fine either way. If we have them, great. If we don't, then he's okay with that too."

"Well, that's good, then. Maybe just relax about it and see what happens. See how you feel?"

Kristen stayed quiet for a long moment before speaking again. "We had a scare last week. I thought I might be pregnant, but I wasn't. I was just late. It freaked me out, though."

Lisa frowned. "Are you still on birth control?"

"I am. That's why I was so confused. I didn't think it

was possible. But then I realized the antibiotic I was taking for a UTI could have interfered with the birth control and I totally panicked until I got the test results. When it came back negative, it was such a huge relief."

"So, that shows you that you're not ready now, and that's okay. Maybe you won't ever be. Or maybe in a few years you'll feel differently. Whatever you want to do, though, is what you should do." Lisa felt a pang of sadness that Kristen might not want children, but quickly pushed the thought away. "I'd love more grandchildren, but your sisters are doing well and I'm sure Chase and Beth will eventually have kids, too."

"They probably will," Kristen agreed. "So, you don't think it's awful if we decide not to have them?"

"No, I don't think it's awful, not at all. You both need to do what feels right."

Kristen sighed and Lisa could see some of the tension leave her. "Thanks, Mom. I was really feeling a little selfish about this. But it is a big decision. And I'm just not sure. All I know is that I'm not ready yet. Maybe I never will be."

Lisa got up and hugged her daughter. "Maybe you won't be. And that's okay. Whatever you decide is okay."

13

———

"*I*'m addicted to this cinnamon tea. Do you want to try a cup?" Lisa asked as her friend Marley settled onto one of the stools around the kitchen island. It was a few minutes past four and her other friends, Sue and Paige were coming for dinner around five thirty. And she'd invited Kay to join them as well.

"That sounds good. It will help me to warm up. It's chilly out there. Suddenly feels like winter today."

Lisa laughed. "It really does. Yet tomorrow they say it might hit 70. You never know this time of year." She poured two cups of hot water and added a delicate silk tea bag to each, brought them over to the island and settled across from Marley.

"What kind of tea is this? It smells heavenly," Marley asked.

"It's Harney's Hot Cinnamon Spice. I got it at Barnes and Noble last time we went off-island and stopped at the Cape Cod Mall. I ordered a cup and liked it so much that I bought a tin. And Amazon sells it too, so I don't have to wait until the next time I go off-island."

Marley nodded. "I like to give the local shops the business as much as possible. But there are times when you can't beat the convenience of online shopping. Speaking of which, let's talk about your sales."

Lisa handed Marley a stack of info she'd asked her to gather and Marley looked through it and had some questions for Lisa. She looked deep in thought and was quiet for a long moment, sipping her tea and staring out the window at the white-tipped waves on the ocean. Finally, she turned to Lisa and smiled.

"Okay, you're going to think I'm crazy, but I have some ideas I want to try. I did some research as well before I came over here. I specifically spent some time on various social media and I looked at what your competitors are doing." She paused and Lisa simply waited for her to continue. Aside from having a Facebook and an Instagram page, Lisa knew very little about social media and how to use it.

"Are you on TikTok? I mean, do you have an account and have you poked around there at all?" Marley asked.

"TikTok? No. Isn't that for young people?" Lisa had heard of it, of course, but that was as far as her knowledge went.

"It started out that way, but one of the top TikTok influencers, Gordon Ramsay, is our age."

Lisa laughed. "Gordon Ramsay is very well known."

"He is. But he's not young, and he has a massively huge following. And he's not the only one. People and businesses of all ages and sizes are on TikTok and when something goes viral there, sales can take off."

Lisa felt confused. "You expect me to post something that will go viral on TikTok to sell my quiches?"

Marley's eyes twinkled. "Yes. Maybe not immediately, maybe not exactly viral, but I would like to see you start having some fun with TikTok. Post short videos that show the inn and your food, closeups of the ingredients, you chopping the lobster, mixing butter into pastry dough, taking the quiches out of the oven....images that will make people's mouths water... and will make them feel like they have to try your quiches now!"

Lisa laughed again. "And you think TikTok can do that?"

"It's hard to imagine if you haven't seen it. So, your assignment for this week is to get on TikTok and start watching videos. There are a ton of food videos—you will probably become addicted pretty quickly. Loads of recipes and travel videos too, all kinds of fun content."

Lisa was doubtful only because she'd never been on the app before, but she trusted Marley's judgement. "Okay, I'll check out TikTok this week. We'll see if I can find a good new recipe or two."

This time Marley laughed. "Oh, you have no idea. Call me Friday afternoon and we'll make a plan."

"Will do. I may need your help though in actually making a video. I have no idea where to start."

"Well, I do. I have a few ideas brewing. We'll discuss on Friday."

"Sounds good. On a different note, how's Mark?" Lisa asked about Marley's fiancé. She'd met him when he engaged her marketing services to help spread the word about his photography business. She hadn't been expecting to find romance on Nantucket and had been pleasantly surprised when they immediately clicked, first as business associates, then as friends, and then more.

Marley smiled at the mention of Mark's name. "Mark is great. He wants to take me to Chatham in a few weeks for my birthday. I've never been there, but he says it's lovely and I know you've mentioned taking a few trips there."

Lisa nodded. "It's my favorite area of the Cape. It reminds me a little of Nantucket with the cute Main Street and shops. There are some great restaurants and we usually stay at the Chatham Bars Inn, which overlooks the ocean."

"I think that's where Mark booked us a room. He wants to take the slow boat over so we can bring our car and do some exploring, maybe take a drive down to Wellfleet and Provincetown."

"I can give you a list of good places to eat in P-town and Wellfleet too. It's a pretty drive. That part of the Cape is less crowded and there are some beautiful beaches. Though it's a little cold now for the beach. There's a great golf course in North Truro that you might enjoy though—it overlooks the ocean and it's not very hard."

Marley looked intrigued. "That might be fun. Mark loves to golf and I'm getting better at it, since I joined that ladies' league last year."

"There's a vineyard not too far from there that might be fun to stop by after you play. Though I'm not sure if it's open this time of year. You could look into it."

"I will. And golfing will depend on the weather too. Maybe we'll get lucky with a sixty or seventy degree day."

"Fingers crossed," Lisa said.

They finished their tea and chatted until the others arrived at five thirty. Lisa popped a lasagna she'd made the night before into the oven to heat up a half hour before they arrived. Paige brought a big Caesar salad and Sue brought a loaf of good sourdough bread from a bakery downtown. Kay brought a big bottle of a red blend that sounded delicious. And Marley had brought bite-sized brownies from the in-house bakery at Stop and Shop.

Lisa poured some of Kay's wine for everyone except Paige, who preferred vodka and soda. Lisa put out a new dip she was curious to get their feedback on. It was a recipe she'd stumbled onto online from The New York Times and it had sounded intriguing—a white bean hummus with coriander and miso. She set a bowl of it on the island, with some crunchy toasted pita chips and celery sticks and raw cauliflower for dipping.

"Is this your parsley hummus that I love?" Marley asked. Lisa often made a dip with lemon, parsley, garlic, and white beans. She hoped this would be as good.

"No, this is a new one. Let me know what you think."

Marley dipped a pita chip in and took a taste. "Oh, it's really good. It has a different taste, that I can't quite place. What is that?"

"Coriander? Or miso?"

"It's delicious," Kay chimed in and Paige and Sue agreed as they all tasted it.

"How did Kristen's studio turn out? You saw it earlier today?" Paige asked.

"I did. Chase did a great job. It turned out lovely. It's bigger than her old studio and has plenty of light. She seems really happy with it."

"Will she sell her cottage?" Paige asked.

"I don't think so. Not right away. She mentioned wanting to try doing Airbnb. We chatted about that a little, too. I gave her some tips for things that have worked well at the inn and how to do some online ads."

"Oh, that's a great idea," Sue said. "Curt wants to Airbnb the apartment over our garage. It has its own entrance, but I'm not sure how I feel about that. It still seems too close to us, maybe." Sue's husband Curt ran an insurance agency in downtown Nantucket and he was very outgoing and well-connected.

"It might not be a bad idea. Curt knows so many people. You might not even need to advertise, and it's always better to rent to people you know."

"I suppose. We'll see. Maybe in the summer."

Lisa plated up the lasagna, and they gathered around the dining room table and chatted for another few hours as they ate, had a bit more wine and enjoyed the brownies Marley brought for dessert. Lisa was glad to see that Kay seemed to be having a good time and fit right in with her friends. She was glad that she seemed to be enjoying her time on Nantucket and was keeping busy.

"Kay, how did you like your first needlepoint class?" Lisa asked.

"It was fantastic. I'm looking forward to next week's class. I got to chatting with Ginny, the woman sitting next to me, and turns out she volunteers at the food pantry too. So, she arranged for me to join her Saturday morning for a shift and she'll show me around. I let Abby know when she called the next day and she added me to the schedule for every other Saturday going forward."

"Oh, that's perfect. I think I've met Ginny at the pantry. Didn't she lose her husband recently?"

Kay nodded. "She did. A few years ago. So we have that in common."

"How are you liking Nantucket so far, Kay?" Sue asked.

Kay smiled. "It's exactly how I'd hoped it would be. Better actually. I didn't expect to meet so many nice people so soon. It feels like a real community here."

"It is a great community," Lisa agreed. "Kay met our neighbor, Walter, and they've been spending time together."

"Walter is good company," Kay said.

"Did you meet his son?" Paige asked. "I read something about him online and realized he was living on the island now."

"I did. And his daughter, Sophie. They were staying with Walter until their house was ready, but it's finished now and they moved in yesterday."

"Chase and his team built Travis's house," Lisa said proudly.

"I bet it's nice," Sue said. "From what I read online, Travis and his company have done very well."

"I wonder if Walter will be glad to have his house back to himself?" Lisa asked.

"I bet it's going to seem awfully quiet. But at least they are nearby. He's thrilled that Travis decided to move back to the island. It's nice to have family nearby."

Lisa knew Kay wished her son wasn't so far away. She

felt grateful that all four of her children were on Nantucket. Kate had moved away for a few years but hadn't gone too far, to Boston. And now she was home. She couldn't imagine how hard it would be to only have one child and to have them live halfway around the world.

14

It was too cold to sit outside in her favorite spot on the porch, so Victoria made do with the sunroom. It was a screened-in room that overlooked the backyard and had nice ocean views. Her parents ate most of their meals there, as it was a comfortable and casual room. It was around ten on Saturday morning and Victoria's mother was out grocery shopping and her father was downtown in his office, so Victoria had the house to herself. She poured herself a fresh cup of coffee, then settled on the sofa, with her computer on her lap.

In her last session, she'd stopped midway through a scene, so it was easy to pick up where she'd left off and she quickly sunk into the story. She finished the scene and immediately dove into the next one and was excited about where the story was going. Before she knew it, her coffee was ice cold and several hours had passed. She was just about finished with her scene when she saw movement out of the corner of her eye.

There was a big moving truck backing into the

driveway next door. The new neighbors were moving in. A moment later, another car pulled into the driveway and Travis got out and walked up to the truck. She watched as he led the way to the front door, unlocked it and the movers began bringing boxes in.

Victoria tried to bring her attention back to her story, but kept getting distracted by the movement outside. It didn't take the movers long as it seemed to mostly be boxes and the occasional small furniture item, like lamps and nightstands. She heard her mother come through the front door and went to help her bring the groceries in.

As they brought the last of the bags inside, the moving truck drove off. Travis stood in the driveway watching them go and waved when he saw Victoria and her mother.

"Welcome," Victoria's mother said. "You're finally moving in. It looks like Chase did a lovely job. Your home is beautiful."

Travis smiled. "Thank you. Yes, he did a great job."

"Mom, do you remember Travis Sturgess? We went to school together."

"Of course. It's nice to see you back on the island. We know your father well. I'm sure he's glad to have you nearby."

"I think he is. Do you want to see inside? Nothing is unpacked yet, of course. But I had the main furniture delivered earlier this week, so it's not totally empty."

"Oh, we'd love to," Victoria's mother said.

As they walked to the front door, Travis explained that while he was living with his father, he bought all new furniture.

"I didn't want to deal with shipping it across the

country and didn't know how long the process would take to build. I would have had to put it all in storage. So it was easier to sell it all before I moved home—and to start fresh."

Victoria imagined that he also didn't want all the memories of his marriage that were bound to be attached to that furniture. She followed her mother and Travis through the front door and was seriously impressed when she stepped inside. The main room was a combination living room and dining room that opened into a big kitchen with an L-shaped counter that had several stools along one side. The ceilings were high and soared to a cathedral with polished hardwood beams. And there were floor to ceiling windows and sliding glass doors that opened onto a deck. The view of the ocean was stunning. They were high on a bluff that overlooked Nantucket sound and it was a windy day, so the waves were bigger than usual.

Travis grinned as he saw them taking in the view. "That's what sold me on this lot. But you have the same view, so you know."

Victoria's mother nodded. "We bought many years ago and when we found this spot, we fell in love with it, too."

"I'll give you the grand tour. Around the corner is my office." He led them to an office that was average size but had a wall of built-in bookcases and the same huge windows looking out at the water. They went upstairs after that and there were four roomy bedrooms, and the master bedroom had French doors that opened to a small deck and a large bathroom with a glass shower and a soaking tub.

Sophie's bedroom was next to Travis' and had a canopy bed with a frilly white top and fluffy pink comforter. "Sophie picked out the bed and colors herself," he said as they looked around the room.

The basement wasn't finished yet, but the house was fully furnished. There were just boxes everywhere.

"Now the fun part begins," Travis said when they returned to the kitchen area. "I left Sophie with my father so I can try to get as much of this done before I bring her back here tonight."

"I don't envy you that. I hate moving. But your place is gorgeous. Once you are all unpacked, it will be awesome," Victoria said.

"I tried to get my dad to move in here with us," Travis said. "I've got two extra bedrooms and I know he had a hard time after my mother died. I think he's liked having us around."

"He doesn't want to move in?" Her mother asked.

Travis shook his head. "He said he's not ready, but thanks, anyway. I guess I don't blame him. He's pretty attached to his house. There's a lot of memories there and he's still in good health."

"And he's not that far away, right?" Victoria asked.

"Right. Nothing is far away on Nantucket, but he's pretty close, just a few miles, and he's on the beach too. He's right by the Beach Plum Cove Inn."

"Lisa Hodges' place. That's a lovely area," Victoria's mother said.

"Right," Travis agreed. "I'm sure he'll be here often, and Sophie will be spending most mornings or afternoons with him, depending on what my days look like. So, we'll see him often. We're all going out to dinner tonight."

"That's good. Your father told us you are still running your business from here. Isn't it something what technology can do?" Victoria's mother said.

Travis grinned. "Yes, it works out pretty well, actually. Except for the time difference. I'm at work hours before my team and they're not all early risers. But it's fine."

"Well, we won't keep you. Thanks for showing us around. If you need anything, we're right next door."

"Thank you." Travis walked them to the door and once they were home, Victoria's mother turned to her. "He seems like a lovely young man. Maybe he's single? Do you know?"

Victoria laughed. "I think he is, actually. But we already dated once and now he's divorced with a kid. I don't think that's a fit for me. You know I've never been into kids."

Her mother looked at her for a long moment before shaking her head. "Hmm. Too bad."

15

"How much longer will you be on Nantucket?" Walter asked. He and Kay were sitting by his window, sipping coffee and watching the waves. It had become part of Kay's routine now—almost every day, as she walked back from the lighthouse, Walter finished up his walk and waved her up for coffee. He was quickly becoming a good friend and Kay was aware that the weeks were going by fast. She'd become a regular for their Thursday Scrabble and pizza nights, too.

"About a month. I was going to leave right before Thanksgiving, but Lisa is trying to convince me to stay and join her family. I don't know what I'm going to do."

"Well, you're welcome to join us, of course, too. We haven't decided if we're going out for dinner or attempting to cook in. Travis has that big fancy kitchen, but neither one of us has ever done the whole meal ourselves."

Kay smiled. "It might be fun to try. You can always get takeout and just cook the turkey yourself. That part is easy."

"That's not a bad idea." Walter frowned at her. "Why would you want to leave before Thanksgiving?"

"It's not that I want to leave. I thought it might be harder to leave if I stay for Thanksgiving, and if I go the week before, I'll miss all the holiday traffic. It's the busiest travel time of the year."

"Well, just think about it then. You don't need to decide yet."

"No, I don't. How are you doing?" Walter had said he was glad to have his house back to himself, but she sensed that he missed having Travis and Sophie around.

Walter ran a hand through his hair and stared out the window for a long moment before speaking. "It's been real quiet since they left. I never noticed that before. I like the quiet. But it was nice having them here." He brightened and smiled. "But they're not far and boy, is his house something. You'll have to see it one of these days."

"It sounds lovely." Walter had shown her pictures, and it looked like a beautiful home. He'd also told her that they'd invited him to live with them there. There was plenty of room. She knew he was tempted, but also understood why the timing wasn't right to make such a big move. Walter's house was lovely too, and it was his and full of memories that he wasn't ready to say goodbye to just yet.

"Tell me more about where you're going from here?" Walter asked.

"I booked a stay at an Airbnb in the historic district of Charleston. It's a big old house that has been divided into six apartments and mine is on the ground floor. It has parking too. I'm not driving down there, so I figured I can just rent a car and explore."

"It will probably be warmer this time of year, I imagine?"

"I hope so! I think it will. I went for a vacation there years ago and have been wanting to go back ever since. There's a lot to see, and the food is wonderful. I plan to have my share of shrimp and grits."

Walter smiled. "You don't see grits much up here."

"No and they're so good, too. I never liked them until I had them in Charleston. The key is adding lots of butter, cheese and cream."

"That makes most things taste better," Walter agreed.

Kay took a sip of her coffee and watched a ferry come into the harbor. She liked that she and Walter were able to sit quietly in comfortable silence. Their conversations were always easy and relaxed.

"Did Travis go on any dates yet from that online place?"

Walter had mentioned that he'd talked his son into putting his profile up on a dating site.

"Not yet, but he has one set up for tomorrow night. He asked if I can watch Sophie for a few hours while he meets her at The Club Car for a drink."

"Oh, how fun! Do you know anything about her?"

"Not much. He said her name is Melissa, or maybe Marie, something like that. Travis wasn't sure he wanted to meet her, and I told him he was crazy not to if she sounded nice. He showed me her picture, and she's a pretty girl, about his age."

"That sounds promising," Kay said.

Walter chuckled. "I may be more excited about the date than he is. But I'm just glad he's getting back out there. He fell too hard for that Kacey. She was all wrong for him, but he didn't know it until he was married. I think he's afraid to make another mistake."

"Well, I hope he has a fun night," Kay said. Thirty-five seemed like another lifetime ago to her. At that age, Travis could find someone wonderful again. She understood his hesitation, though. At her age, she couldn't imagine wanting to date again.

She glanced at Walter, and he looked content as he lifted his coffee mug and took a sip. She'd had men ask her out in recent months, people she knew from church or the senior center. Lovely men but she wasn't interested in any of them. She was glad that Walter hadn't done anything silly like ask her for a date. She could tell he felt the same as she did, and was just happy to have a new friend.

16

*T*ravis arrived at The Club Car restaurant at ten minutes before five. He'd suggested five o'clock as a meeting time because if the drink went well, then he could suggest dinner and still be home early for Sophie. It was also early enough that the bar wasn't packed and there were plenty of open seats. He sat in one that faced the door so he could spot Michelle when she arrived. He ordered a glass of water while he waited and checked his phone when it chimed to announce a new text message. It was from his father.

"Good luck tonight. Remember, it's just a date. Try to relax and have fun."

Travis shook his head. His father was so eager to see him dating. "Thanks. Will do."

"Is she there yet?"

Travis laughed. "No, or I wouldn't be texting you."

"Good! That would be rude."

Travis was still smiling when he glanced toward the front door and saw a pretty woman walk in and look around the bar. She had shoulder-length blonde hair and was wearing a light blue sleeveless dress and a dark blue jacket. Her gaze stopped when she reached him and she smiled. It was Michelle.

He'd sent his picture over after they'd exchanged initial messages, and he was glad to see that she looked just like her photo. Sometimes they didn't. He'd gone on a date before he met Kacey and the woman that showed up looked very different from the picture she'd posted online. He stood and waved her over.

"Travis?"

He nodded and gave her a quick hug. "It's nice to meet you."

Michelle slid into the seat next to him.

"What would you like to drink?" He asked as the bartender appeared to take their order.

"I'll have a Pinot Grigio, thanks."

"A Whales Tale IPA for me." It was his favorite, and he also liked to support the local brewery.

The bartender brought their drinks, and they both took a sip. Travis felt nervous for a moment. First dates could be awkward and the conversation didn't always flow easily. But after a few minutes of back and forth get-to-know you conversation, he relaxed a bit. Michelle seemed easy enough to talk to.

"Tell me more about your daughter?" She asked. "Is she three or four, I think you said?"

That just won her a brownie point. Sophie was his favorite subject.

"She's four and I know I'm biased since I'm her dad, but

she seems incredibly smart for her age. She's with my dad right now."

Michelle smiled, and he noticed that her eyes were brown but with a hint of green. "That's the best kind of babysitter. So, your parents still live on the island? And you grew up here?"

"I did. It's just my dad now. My mother passed a few years ago."

"Oh, I'm sorry to hear that." Michelle took a sip of wine and looked around the restaurant, which was suddenly filling up now that it was a little past five and people were out of work. "So, you went to college and then moved home?"

"Eventually, yes." Travis was intentionally vague. "Tell me more about your job. I think you said you travel often?"

"I do. I work in pharmaceutical sales, and travel all over New England. My grandmother passed a few years ago, and we decided to keep her house here. My parents come for a month or two in the summer and I'm here as often as possible year-round, depending on my travel schedule. I have an apartment just outside Boston as well. That is often easier during the week."

"I bet. I love it here, but it's not always convenient if you have to get off-island quickly."

"Do you travel at all, or are you able to totally work remotely?"

"I hate to travel and I can't really now, with Sophie. Though I suppose if I had to, my father could watch her for a few days. But, I don't really need to go anywhere."

Michelle looked intrigued. "What do you do exactly? Something in tech?"

Travis debated how much to share and decided to say as little as possible. "I work in marketing for a software company." He decided to change the subject away from work stuff.

"Tell me more about you. What do you like to do when you're not working?" He asked.

Michelle smiled. "I run most mornings. It's a great stress-reliever and gets me energized for the day. I love the beach and going out to restaurants and to hear live music. What about you?"

"I love the beach, too. I'm not great at it, but I like surfing. And fishing. And spending time with Sophie."

"You sound like a devoted dad," Michelle said.

"I am. Sophie's my whole world." He explained about Kacey and that she wasn't around much. Michelle seemed surprised.

"Oh, so you have full custody? That's unusual these days."

"It's the best thing, for Sophie and for me."

Michelle took a sip of her wine. "She's lucky to have you."

"Thanks. Are you hungry? We could grab a bite to eat if you like?"

"I'd love that."

The bartender brought over menus and they decided to split an order of queso dip with chips for an appetizer. Michelle ordered pan-seared chicken and Travis went with a burger. They made a great burger at The Club Car and Travis wanted something more casual.

Over dinner, Travis couldn't find one thing wrong with Michelle. If he'd had a list, she would have checked all the boxes. She was pretty, easy to talk to, seemed successful and, more importantly, happy with her job and she said she liked kids. She'd told him about how she loved to watch her sister's kids.

"Jane has two girls, five and seven, and they're just the sweetest things. She and her husband live near me and I often watch the girls for a night so they can get out and have a break."

Travis nodded. "That's nice of you. As much as I love Sophie, I need to get out now and then, too."

When he met Kacey for the first time, he'd had such an intensely physical reaction to her—like nothing he'd ever experienced. He'd never been in love before and it hit him hard and right away. Though in retrospect, he realized now it wasn't love at first sight as much as lust at first sight. And lust fades. Love endures. Or at least he liked to think that real love would. If there was such a thing.

So, he didn't have that same immediate attraction to Michelle. He might be suspicious if he had. And it might have scared him off. Dinner went well. They laughed and enjoyed their food and after he paid the bill, and suggested they do it again soon, he was encouraged that Michelle agreed immediately. Her smile was warm, and she held his gaze as he said goodbye to her. And he suddenly felt awkward again. He was out of practice. What was the custom these days on a first date? Was a kiss expected? Too forward? He hesitated just long enough that it would have been more awkward if he initiated a kiss at that point. So, he instead leaned in and gave her a quick goodbye hug.

"This was fun. Thank you for coming out. Can I walk you to your car?"

Michelle grinned. "Thank you for dinner. I got lucky. My car is right there." She glanced toward a white BMW convertible that was parked as close to The Club Car as possible. Travis was parked in the opposite direction.

"Alright, I'll say goodbye then. I'll call you soon, and we'll make a plan."

"Goodnight, Travis. I look forward to it."

17

The next day, when Victoria got home from the newspaper, it was a little after six, and she was starving. Her parents were out to dinner with friends, and she figured she'd look through the fridge and probably end up eating leftover pasta or heating up a can of soup. As she was about to step inside, she saw a package by the door and picked it up. She assumed it was either a pair of shoes she'd ordered online or something for her mother. But the package was addressed to Travis Sturgess. UPS had delivered to the wrong house. She unlocked the front door and tossed her bag and computer inside. Then grabbed the box to bring it to her new neighbor.

When she reached the front door, she knocked lightly. She could see through the glass window that Travis and his daughter Sophie were in the kitchen. Travis turned at the sound of her knocking and opened the door a moment later.

Victoria held up the box. "This was delivered to us by mistake."

"Thank you." Travis took the box from her and opened the door wider. "Do you want to come in for a minute?"

Victoria was about to say no as her stomach was rumbling. But then she smelled it. The intoxicating scent of hot cheese pizza. Travis grinned. "We were just about to have some pizza and there's too much for the two of us. Are you hungry?"

"I could stay for a slice. Thanks." Saying no to that pizza wasn't an option. Victoria followed Travis into the kitchen, where Sophie was getting paper plates from a drawer.

"Sophie, this is our neighbor, Victoria. She's going to have some pizza with us."

Sophie handed her a paper plate. "Do you like pizza?"

Victoria smiled. "I love it!"

Sophie grinned back and scampered off to get her pizza.

Travis opened the box, and the scent intensified. It was a large pizza, half cheese and half pepperoni. He put two slices of cheese pizza on Sophie's plate, then asked Victoria what she'd like. "I usually start with one of each," he said.

"That sounds good to me," Victoria agreed.

Once they all had their pizza, they took their plates to a big round table next to the kitchen and by a gas fireplace. If it wasn't getting dark already, the view of the ocean would have been spectacular.

"What would you like to drink? We have water, root beer, regular beer or I think I have some wine somewhere, too."

"Root beer sounds good, actually."

"That's what I'm having!" Sophie lifted her pink sippy cup and took a sip.

"Root beer all around, then." Travis returned a moment later with their drinks, and Victoria gratefully took a bite of cheese pizza. It was from one of her favorite local places, Foggy Island Pizza.

"Are you all settled in now?" Victoria didn't see any packing boxes anywhere.

"Pretty much. I still have some things ordered, but it's small stuff like lamps and prints to hang on the wall. All the unboxing is done."

"And I helped," Sophie said with enthusiasm.

Victoria smiled. Sophie was well-behaved and cute. She could see the resemblance to Travis. They both had the same wavy hair and deep brown eyes.

"Sophie was a big help," Travis confirmed.

Victoria inhaled her two slices of pizza and didn't say no when Travis offered a third.

"Daddy, can I go watch SpongeBob?" Sophie squirmed in her seat, eager to run off. She still had half a slice of pizza left.

"Two more bites first."

"Okay." She took two tiny bites, then ran off to watch TV.

As soon as Sophie left the table, Travis's cell phone rang. He glanced at it, then picked it up. "Sorry, I need to take this real quick." He answered and said, "Hi Dad, is everything ok?"

She picked up a hint of worry in his voice. But then he chuckled. "No, I haven't called her yet. Yes, I will. I'll see you in the morning."

He ended the call and took a big bite of pizza while

Victoria wondered who Travis was supposed to call. She didn't ask though, as it was none of her business.

"Sorry about that," Travis said. "My father watched Sophie last night while I went on my first date in a long time. I think he was more excited about it than I was."

"Someone you met online?" That explained why she hadn't heard anything further from the person who contacted her, who she was pretty sure was Travis.

"Yeah, I messaged with a few people and Michelle was the first one I exchanged pictures with. We met for a drink and a bite to eat at The Club Car. She seems nice enough."

Victoria laughed. "You don't sound all that interested."

"I think I'm just out of practice. There's nothing wrong with her. She's pretty and smart and we had fun. I just didn't feel a big spark like I did with my former wife. But I liked her enough to want to take her out again and see if it can grow. They say that's better sometimes—for things to go slower, get to really know a person first and let the attraction build."

"I don't think anyone really knows what's best," Victoria said. "I was with Todd for so long. Part of me dreads dating again. I don't really know how to do it."

"You haven't been bombarded with men on that site?" Travis sounded surprised. "I thought you would have had your pick of dates."

"I didn't put a picture up either. I've had a few responses, but nothing memorable yet."

"Well, don't give up. I had a friend that did a trial month on one of those sites and on the last day when he was about to cancel, he got a message from someone that caught his interest. She seemed almost too good to be true. They had so much in common. He was sure she'd be disappointing in person, that they wouldn't have any chemistry."

"But they did?" Victoria leaned forward, eager to hear what happened.

"He said when they met, it was like they'd known each other for ages. The conversation flowed so easily. They stayed up until one talking non-stop. He said it was like they hadn't seen each other and were rushing to catch-up. He knew instantly that she was the one. And I guess she felt the same way because three weeks later they moved in together and three months later they got married."

"Wow."

"I know. After Kacey, anything that intense would scare me off, I think. Or at least make me very wary. Ordinarily, I would think you need to know someone longer. But they made it work. Ten years later and they're still happily married and have twin eight-year-old boys."

"That's a great story. You just never know," Victoria said. Her pizza was gone, and both she and Travis had empty plates. She stood. "Well, I should probably get going. I don't want to keep you. Thanks for the pizza."

Travis grinned. "Anytime." He glanced toward the living room. "Sophie, come say goodbye to Victoria."

A moment later, Sophie flew across the room and gave Victoria a big hug. "Will you come back for pizza again?" The enthusiastic question took her by surprise. Victoria smiled at both of them. "Sure. I can't say no to pizza."

"Who can?" Travis joked. He walked her to the door.

"Thanks for dinner."

"Thank you for bringing that package over. See you soon."

18

A WEEK LATER.

"Are you excited about your date?" Taylor asked.

It was almost five on a Thursday and Victoria and Taylor were finishing up in the office and Victoria was far from excited for her first date.

Inspired by Travis, after having pizza with him and Sophie, Victoria checked her messages on the dating site. She'd quickly deleted three that were either much too old or just not interesting, but there were two that had promise. She exchanged a few messages with each over the next day or so and sent her photos to both.

She knew it would be impossible to really tell until she met them in person, but they were both attractive and, based on their profiles, they shared some common interests. One of them, Richard, was at a sales conference on the West Coast and wouldn't be back for a week, but they agreed to set something up when he returned.

The other, Brad, suggested meeting after work at the Rose and Crown for a drink and she liked that idea. It was an easy walk from the office and it was a casual place with good pub food.

"I'm more dreading it than excited, to be honest," Victoria admitted.

Taylor looked sympathetic. "It's not easy to get back out there. And first dates are always awkward. It's probably just as intimidating for him, too. Try to think of it as just meeting someone interesting—have an after-work drink and go from there, no expectations." She paused for a moment before adding, "Maybe he'll just be a new friend... or he could be the love of your life." Taylor finished on a dramatic and hopeful note and Victoria couldn't help but laugh.

"I'll focus on a drink with a new friend. Do I look okay?" She'd tried on a half-dozen outfits that morning trying to figure out the best thing to wear for both work and a casual drinks date. She finally settled on dark jeans, her favorite chocolate brown leather boots and a flattering soft pink sweater with a v-neck.

"You look great! I love that color on you. It makes your skin glow," Taylor said.

"Thanks. Well, I guess it's time. Wish me luck." Victoria shut down her computer and grabbed her purse.

"Good luck. If you get home early, call me. Can't wait to hear how it goes."

"I will."

Victoria headed out the door and walked the short distance to the Rose and Crown. It was just a few streets away from the office. She'd told Brad she'd meet him there at 5:15 and it was exactly that time when she reached the front door. The Rose and Crown was a popular after-work spot and it was already getting busy. She stepped inside tentatively and glanced toward the bar and felt a mix of relief and nervousness when she spotted Brad. The bar was filling up, but he'd found a seat and there was an empty one beside him.

Victoria made her way over to the bar. Brad smiled when he spotted her and stood when she reached him. He held out his hand. "Victoria? Nice to meet you."

She smiled and shook his hand. Brad's grip was firm and confident. That was a good start. She slid into the seat next to him and he sat back down.

"I just ordered a draft beer, what would you like?" He asked as the bartender set his drink down.

"I'll have a cabernet, Josh, if you have it?"

The bartender nodded and a moment later returned with her wine.

Victoria's worry that there would be awkward silences was a non-issue. Brad immediately started talking... about himself.

He told her all about the condo he just bought on the waterfront, and how much he paid for it, then launched right into telling her all about his job and how good he was at it.

He sat up tall in his seat and it was clear he was quite impressed with himself and expected her to be as well. "I'm a senior trader at a hedge fund company. Started there two years ago and have already been promoted twice."

That was impressive, though. Victoria could respect someone being driven and ambitious and doing well in their career. "That's great. I didn't realize there was a hedge fund here on Nantucket. Usually they're in Boston or New York."

Brad took a sip of his beer. "The company headquarters are in Boston. One partner lives there and runs that office and the other is here. He used to be in Boston, too, and had a summer place here, then just decided to be here full time."

"And you like being here rather than Boston?"

Brad grinned. "It's Nantucket. What's not to like? I used to spend my summers here too, shared a house with a bunch of guys. I graduated from Boston College and did a summer internship at their Boston office. When I graduated, they made me an offer, and I got to choose which location. It's pretty sweet to do this on Nantucket."

Victoria smiled. She liked his enthusiasm, and it was clear that he loved Nantucket, which she also appreciated.

"And the money is insane," Brad continued. "My year-end bonus will be more than most people's salaries. And the longer I stay with the company, the more my comp will increase. In a few years, I'll be getting seven-figure bonuses and profit sharing. That's where the real money is. I just bought a sweet new car—a red Lamborghini." He looked very pleased with himself. But the more he bragged about how much money he made and was going to make, the more she wished she was home in her sweats, eating a bowl of ice cream.

"That's nice."

"It's a car that people pay attention to."

"I'm sure." Victoria glanced at the time on her cellphone. She'd only been there for fifteen minutes. Time was going by very slowly.

"So, when you're not working, what do you like to do for fun?" She tried to change the subject.

"I'm a believer in working hard and playing hard. So I'm out most nights. I love hearing live bands and I like my cocktails. I have a pretty high tolerance though. I can go out most nights and still get to work on time in the morning without too much of a hangover."

Victoria was horrified and wondered if it showed. She forced a smile. "If I have more than two glasses of wine, I'm usually regretting it the next day—especially if it's a work night."

"You gotta build up to it. It's like a muscle. Just need to get your body used to it."

Victoria glanced at her watch again and took another sip of her wine. She definitely did not want a second drink.

"Speaking of drinks, you ready for another?" Brad took the last sip of his beer and waved the bartender over.

"Another beer for me." He glanced at Victoria and she put her hand over her almost empty glass.

"I'm good, thanks. I have to get going soon, actually."

Brad looked disappointed. "You can't stay? I thought maybe we'd get a bite to eat, have a few more drinks."

But Victoria couldn't wait to leave. "I'm sorry. I only planned for a quick drink. I have dinner plans with my parents." That wasn't totally a lie. She would eat at home with her parents—though they may be on dessert by the time she got home. She stood and put her hand out. "It was really great to meet you, Brad."

He shook her hand and motioned for her to put her

money away when she took a twenty-dollar bill out of her wallet.

"Your drink is on me. Maybe next time, you'll let me buy you dinner?"

Victoria smiled. "Thanks so much. Have a great night, Brad."

When Victoria arrived home, her parents were just sitting down to eat. Her father was halfway through a vodka martini with a twist, his usual cocktail of choice, while her mother was sipping a Southern Comfort Manhattan on the rocks. They usually just had one drink before dinner, and after tasting both years ago, Victoria understood why. She hadn't told her parents about the date as she didn't want to answer questions from her mother, who would be enthusiastically hopeful and eager to hear how things went.

"Perfect timing, honey. Help yourself to a plate. The pasta is in the oven."

When she'd first moved home, Victoria decided to join her parents for cocktail hour and tasted each one, not sure which she'd prefer. As it turned out, she hated both of them. The vodka martini just tasted like lemon-scented vodka and she'd never acquired a liking for vodka—unless it was hidden by fruit juices or other flavorings. Her mother's Manhattan was even worse—Victoria didn't think could ever like that. She'd chosen wine ever since.

She poured herself a half glass of cabernet and scooped some baked ziti onto a plate, then joined her parents at the dinner table.

"How was your day? Any interesting stories you're working on?" Her father asked.

She smiled, tempted to tell them about Brad, but knew that would get her mother too interested in future dating updates. She hadn't asked in a while and it was nice not feeling that pressure. Victoria knew her mother meant well and just wanted to see her happy—but to her generation, that meant being part of a couple, ideally married or engaged.

"It was a quiet day. Nothing exciting going on. What's new with you two?"

After dinner, she called Taylor to fill her in.

"Are you sure he was that bad? You used to be impressed when Todd told you about his real estate deals," Taylor reminded her.

"That was different. Todd never bragged about how much money he made. I always asked him for details on his properties because it was interesting and I was impressed by how hard he worked. He never liked that kind of attention—he wasn't flashy about it like Brad. Todd drove an old Jeep he bought second-hand."

"Maybe he was nervous and just trying to impress you?" Taylor wasn't ready to give up on Brad yet. But Victoria hadn't told her about the drinking yet. When she did, Taylor conceded and moved on.

"Okay, Brad's out. So, when are you meeting Richard?"

Victoria laughed. "We haven't set a date yet. When he gets back from his trip, we are supposed to touch base. Though honestly, after Brad, I'm not so sure I want to go through this again."

"You have to. What if he's great? He can't possibly be worse than Brad, right?"

19

*K*ay arrived at the food pantry a few minutes before nine on Saturday morning. They didn't officially open until ten, but Abby had emailed the night before and suggested that she and Ginny arrive an hour early to start packing the orders, as there were a few more than usual. Abby's role with the pantry was as one of the five volunteer co-managers. She also took orders by phone Thursday afternoon and Friday morning for the Saturday shift.

Ginny was punching in the key code to the pantry front door as Kay walked up. Abby had dropped the order sheets off Friday afternoon and they divided them up and each took five orders. Like other food pantries Kay had volunteered with, this pantry was entirely self-funded by donations from individuals and corporations. They received most of their food once a month from the Greater Boston Food Bank and there were strong volunteers that showed up every time to unload and carry the food into the pantry.

There was no typical profile for the clients that frequented the pantry. They were allowed to place an order as often as once a week, and many did. The policy of the pantry, like most, was that they didn't ask a lot of questions—if someone showed up and said they needed food, they happily gave it to them.

Some of the people shared that they were in between jobs and having a hard time getting by, while others were from other countries, working in the kitchens or hotels or whatever job they could get. Affordable housing was always a problem on Nantucket. Some employers provided it, but many did not and many of their clients struggled to get by, especially those with children.

Kay and Ginny spent the next hour putting the orders together so they would be ready when the clients arrived at their scheduled time, fifteen minutes apart. They added juice, milk, canned goods, peanut butter, pasta, rice, soups, cereals, toilet paper, condiments, fresh fruits and vegetables and frozen meats to the various orders. Most of the food were staples, but there was also the occasional treat— a bag of chips or box of cookies.

Kay added an extra bag of frozen strawberries to Claire Smith's bag. Her husband, Alan, was very ill and Claire had to puree everything for him and he loved strawberries. When Kay handed her the bag, Claire took a peek inside and smiled gratefully. "Alan is in for a treat. Thanks a million."

Most of the clients were like Claire, appreciative of whatever the pantry gave them. But there were a few who struggled with other issues, mental illness or alcohol or drug addiction, and these clients would sometimes place an order and then not show up or seem out of it when they did arrive.

One such regular, Carlos, pulled up on his bicycle with an empty backpack. He slurred his words slightly as Ginny helped him put his food order into his backpack. Still, he was polite as he thanked them and rode off on his bike, wobbling just a little at first.

Ginny shook her head. "He was doing so well for months. Told me he'd been attending AA meetings. And he's so young. Just turned thirty-eight last month."

"Maybe it's just a temporary setback," Kay said. "If he attended in the past, hopefully he'll find his way back." She'd seen many clients at her old pantry that alternated between months or years attending meetings and staying sober to periods of time when they gave in to their demons and drank or used drugs again.

"I hope so."

The rest of the shift went by quickly and when they finished, Kay followed Ginny to Dover Falls, the retirement community where she lived. She'd invited Kay to come for lunch, along with a few of her other friends. Kay parked and followed Ginny into her unit, which was a lovely and spacious condo with a deck and distant view of the ocean.

Ginny gave her a tour and showed her the two bedrooms, one a spacious primary bedroom with an attached bathroom and French doors that opened to another smaller deck. Her living area had a cathedral ceiling and a gas fireplace and was a bright open space with an adjoining cozy kitchen and dining area. It was nothing like what Kay had imagined a retirement community would look like.

"This is so nice. How long have you lived here?" Kay asked as Ginny went to the kitchen and took a big tossed salad out of the refrigerator and set it on the counter.

"Jim and I moved here ten years ago. The stairs were getting hard for him and we had friends that lived here and loved it. They raved about not having to worry about stairs or shoveling snow or cutting the lawn or any of that. I know you can get that in a regular condo too, but here it's more geared to our needs." Ginny went back to the refrigerator and took a bowl of lobster salad out. She opened a bag of crusty rolls, sliced them in half, spread a little butter on the cut surface and put them on a tray to toast in the oven.

"I'll wait until the girls arrive to actually toast them. It will only take a few minutes and they're better when they are warm."

"It would be nice to not worry about shoveling snow," Kay said. "I have thought about downsizing and moving into a condo. I just hate the idea of change, I guess."

"It is hard to let go, and it's a big decision to move, whether it's to a condo or a retirement community. We thought about a regular condo, but we didn't want to have to move again in a few years. Here, we have the benefits of a condo but also they provide all of our meals, so we don't have to worry about cooking. And the food is excellent. The chef came from one of the top restaurants on the island."

Kay was impressed and surprised. "That sounds

wonderful, but I wonder why he would make a move like that?"

"I asked him. I wondered too. But once he told me, it made sense. When you're a chef in a busy restaurant, it means long hours and most nights and holidays away from your family. Here he can work on a more normal schedule. Dinner is served at four thirty and after that he can go home to his wife and relax."

"Oh, that does make sense. I imagine years of working nights and holidays must get old after a while."

Ginny nodded. "Yes, and another thing we liked about it here is that eventually if we need it, there are assisted living services and even a memory care wing. My husband passed so suddenly that we never used those services. Hopefully I won't need them—but you never know."

Kay thought of a friend she knew, whose memory had declined suddenly when she turned eighty and six months later, she had to go into a memory care unit as she was living alone. She shuddered at the thought but could see how a place like Dover Falls would be appealing, even if those services weren't needed when you moved in.

"It does sound nice to have all your meals provided. I used to love to cook for Al, but it's just not the same cooking for one."

"It's really not. But it's still fun for me to cook now and then when I have people over."

The doorbell rang, and Ginny opened the door.

"Carol and Patty are here!"

"We rode over together," Carol said as they walked inside. Ginny introduced them to Kay, and they all gathered in the kitchen. Ginny popped the tray of rolls in the oven and asked what they'd all like to drink. "I have herbal tea, water, or I could make us mimosas."

"Mimosas, of course!" Carol said, and they all laughed and agreed. Ginny got out four champagne flutes and opened a bottle of Prosecco that was chilling in the refrigerator. She filled each glass a little more than halfway, then added a splash of orange juice and a drop of Chambord, a raspberry liquor. Kay had never had a mimosa with Chambord, and it was delicious.

A few minutes later, Ginny took the rolls out of the oven and piled a generous mound of lobster salad on each one and put out four plates so everyone could help themselves to a lobster roll and some salad. They took their food to the dining room table and Kay enjoyed both the delicious lobster and the conversation.

Carol and Patty had been friends with Ginny for years, but after just a few minutes, Kay felt like she'd known them longer, too. They were funny and welcoming and they all loved to dish the gossip about people they knew on the island.

"Did you see Muriel has taken up with her golf instructor, Roman? He's literally half her age. I wonder what he sees in her?" Patty said.

"Muriel Summers? Isn't she our age? So if she's seventy-two, he's thirty-six? That can't be right," Carol said.

"Okay, so maybe not literally. But I think he's in his mid-fifties," Patty said.

"I can think of a reason," Ginny said archly.

"Is she very rich?" Kay asked. She assumed that's what Ginny meant.

Ginny nodded. "Insanely. Her husband passed a few

years ago, and they used to live in a Manhattan penthouse apartment when they weren't at their Hamptons estate. He did something in financial services. Rumor is she's worth close to a billion. She sold all the other properties when he passed and moved here. Though I think she may buy something in Florida. She told me just last week when I saw her at the club that she's tired of the cold winters here. I did not know about Roman, though. That is intriguing."

"Good for her. She seems happy. She's also savvier than people think. If Roman is after her money, I don't think he'll have an easy time getting his hands on it," Patty said.

Patty was feisty and Kay liked her immediately. Carol too. She knew from what Ginny had told her that Patty still worked as a realtor and did very well. She knew just about everyone in town. She also drove a red BMW convertible and was madly in love with a widower her age that she'd met a year ago at the club. Carol was the only one that was still married. She was quieter and Ginny had said her husband was the outgoing one. They both loved to golf, so they played often.

"Do you golf, Kay?" Carol asked.

Kay shook her head. "No. It does look fun, though."

"It's a fabulous sport," Carol said. "Good exercise and it's a fun social thing, too. You should think about taking some lessons and maybe joining a ladies' league. It's a great way to meet people."

"That's how I met my Tony," Patty said. "There was a party at the club after a charity tournament and silent auction. We both bid on the same item, tickets to the US Open, and he came over to congratulate me. I liked him immediately and invited him to go with me. And we've been together ever since!"

Kay smiled. "That's wonderful. I'll think about that once I'm back home."

Patty frowned. "Oh, that's right, you're just here temporarily. Where do you live?"

"Arlington, just outside Boston. I'm heading to Charleston though when I leave here and after that, I'm not sure. Maybe I'll keep going south and spend some time in Florida over the winter. I'm playing it by ear."

"Well, that sounds like a fun adventure," Patty said.

They spent the next hour laughing and chatting as they moved on from lunch to dessert, when Ginny set out a plate of assorted bite-sized cheesecakes. And herbal tea.

"Did you make these?" Carol asked.

Ginny laughed. "No. I bought them at the market. I haven't baked in years."

Kay had two mini-cheesecakes, one topped with cherries, and one with a caramel and pecan topping. Both were delicious, but by the time she left and walked out with Patty and Carol, she was completely stuffed and slightly sleepy from the one mimosa and so much food.

Patty and Carol hugged her goodbye as they reached their cars. "It was great meeting you," Kay said.

"You too," they both said at once. "Hopefully, we'll see you again before you leave for Charleston," Patty said.

"I hope so, too."

20

When Kay turned her car into the driveway at the inn, she was very tempted to go upstairs and take a nap. She wasn't much for naps, though, as she usually found herself unable to get to sleep later that night. So, even though her bed was calling to her, with the soft comforter and fluffy pillows, she stifled a yawn and looked out the window. It was almost four, but it was still sunny and maybe she could walk off some of her lunch and sleepiness with a walk along the beach.

She set her purse down, grabbed her keys and cell-phone, pulled on her warmest hat and headed outside.

The beach was mostly empty, as it was late in the day. But there were still a few people out walking their dogs. As she reached Walter's house, something red caught her eye in the sand by his steps. As she got closer, she realized it was his Red Sox baseball cap and Walter was wearing it and laying in the sand. She ran over to him and he turned his head as she drew closer and slowly sat up. He looked confused and dazed.

"Walter, what happened? Did you fall down your steps?" She realized as she asked it, though, that he was too far from the steps to have fallen from there.

Walter squinted and took a moment before answering. "I don't know exactly. I guess I must have passed out. I came outside to take a walk on the beach. Had an extra hotdog with my beans at lunch and felt like moving around a little. Next thing I knew, I'm lying here and woke up to see you."

Kay tried not to sound too alarmed, but she was very concerned. "Do you know how long you were out?"

He shook his head. "I'm not sure. I left my phone on the kitchen table and didn't check the time before I left, and I don't know what time it is now."

Kay pulled out her phone. "It's almost a quarter past four."

"Hmm. I'm sorry, I still don't know. But I feel okay. Want to come in and have a cup of coffee or tea? I know you prefer your tea late in the day."

Kay knew if she hadn't come alone when she did, that Walter would have done exactly that, nothing. He would have gone inside and made himself a coffee and not said a word about it again. It made her wonder something.

"Walter, has this ever happened before?"

"Yeah, now that you mention it. It happened a few weeks ago too. I was home, though. I'd just gotten out of the shower and had sat on my bed to put my socks on and next thing I knew, I woke up a short time later. Didn't think much of it at the time. Figured I was just tired."

"Walter, we're going to the ER. Please call Travis and

tell him to meet us there." She handed him his phone and glared at him, daring him to say no.

"I don't want to make a big fuss. I feel fine. Can't I just call my doctor tomorrow?"

"No. It's not normal to pass out like that, Walter. You need to be seen to rule out anything serious or heart-related."

"Okay. I suppose it can't hurt to get checked out."

"Travis would want you to go."

Walter chuckled. "Yes, he would. I'll get my cell phone."

He went inside and returned a moment later with his phone.

"Call Travis," Kay said as they walked toward her car.

Walter dialed his son and asked him to meet them at the hospital.

"I'm sure it's nothing serious. But Kay is insisting."

*S*ophie was playing with her dolls in the living room while Travis sat on the sofa, working on his laptop, when his father called and asked him to meet him and Kay at the hospital. His father had assured him it was nothing serious, and he sounded like he thought Kay was overreacting, but Travis liked Kay and doubted that was the case. He knew that ERs were always busy though, and they were likely to be there for hours before they were seen or had any answers. He didn't want to drag Sophie there for that length of time.

"Sophie, I'll be right back. I'm going to run next door and talk to Victoria's mom for a minute."

Sophie was very intent on her tea party with her dolls and didn't even look up. "Okay."

Travis walked across his driveway to the house next door and noticed that there was only one car in the driveway and he thought it was Victoria's. He hoped that her mother was home. He knocked on the door and a moment later, Victoria answered. She was wearing jeans, and an old faded red sweatshirt that said Nantucket across the front. Her hair was twisted up into a messy bun and she had a pen stuck through it. She looked distracted, as though she'd been deep into something and he'd interrupted.

"Hey there. I'm sorry to bother you. Is your mom home, by any chance?"

Victoria frowned. "My mother? No. She and my dad are visiting friends. Can I help you with something? What did you need my mother for?"

Travis hesitated. "She'd mentioned that if I ever needed someone to watch Sophie, to let her know. I hadn't planned on taking her up on it, but my father just called and he's going to the ER and I wanted to meet him there. I'm not sure what to do now. I guess I'll just bring Sophie with me."

"Hello, I'm here. I'd be happy to watch her. It's no problem at all."

She sounded sincere, but still he hesitated. "I don't want to interrupt your day. It was your mom that offered."

"Travis, don't be silly. Your father is in the hospital. Of course I don't mind. I hope he's okay?"

"Thanks. He doesn't think it's anything serious, but his

neighbor found him passed out on the beach and he has no idea how that happened."

"Oh, that's a little scary. I'm glad they are going to get checked out."

"I am too. I'll go get Sophie and bring her over." He took a step back and went to walk back to his house.

"Wait a minute. I'll come with you. It's easier for Sophie to stay home, I would imagine. I'll just grab my laptop."

"Were you working? Are you sure you don't mind?"

Victoria laughed. "It's not work. I'm just playing around at writing fiction. It's just for fun."

She ran inside and returned a moment later with her laptop, and they walked over to the house.

"I didn't know you write fiction."

"This is new. Like I said, though, it's just for fun."

"Well, you never know when a fun hobby could turn into something more," Travis said. He grinned as they reached his front door. "That's how I started my company —I was just having fun, too. When you love what you do, it doesn't feel like work."

He stepped inside and held the door open for Victoria to follow. "Sophie, we're back. Look who came to see you?"

That got Sophie to look up and when she saw it was Victoria, she broke into a big smile and ran over to them.

"Hi Victoria! Do you want to see my dolls?"

Victoria smiled. "Sure."

"Sophie, Victoria's going to visit with you for a while. I have to go out for a little while." He debated whether to share that her grandfather was in the hospital. Sophie was sensitive, and he didn't want to worry her unnecessarily. But Sophie was hardly paying attention. She'd grabbed

Victoria's hand and was pulling her into the living room where her dolls were.

"I'll be back soon." Travis jotted his cell phone number on a scrap of paper. "In case you need it, I left my number by the door," he called out. Victoria gave him a wave, and he went on his way.

21

"Can we make cookies?"

The question took Victoria by surprise. Sophie was apparently done playing with her dolls.

Victoria hadn't made cookies in years. But it was one of the few things she felt confident doing in the kitchen.

"I don't know. How do you think your father would feel about that?" What if Travis were to come home, and the kitchen was a disaster, with flour and cookies everywhere? Though realistically, they had plenty of time. He was likely to be gone for several hours, at least.

"Daddy loves cookies. We make them sometimes. I can show you how. It's easy!"

Victoria laughed. "What kind did you want to make?"

Sophie gave her a look like she'd asked the most stupid question ever.

"Chocolate chip, of course! We just follow the recipe on the back of the bag. That's what Daddy does. I can't read yet, but I know what goes in the cookies."

She ran to the kitchen and opened the cupboard, and

put a bag of chocolate chips on the counter. Then she got a box of butter and a carton of eggs from the refrigerator and went back to a different cupboard for flour, sugar, baking soda and vanilla.

"I think that is everything, but you should check to be sure."

Victoria picked up the bag of chocolate chips and flipped it over. "The only thing we are missing is salt. Good job, Sophie!" She turned on the oven.

Sophie beamed, then went looking in the cupboard for the salt and added it to the collection on the counter.

"Okay, we need two bowls," Victoria said. "A big mixing bowl and a smaller one for the dry ingredients. Where would I find bowls?"

"Up there." Sophie pointed to a cupboard by the sink. Victoria opened it and found the bowls she needed. Sophie meanwhile got utensils out of a drawer and then they got to work. Victoria showed Sophie how to lightly crack an egg on the side of the bowl, pry it open, and drop the egg into the bowl. Sophie tried it and only got one tiny piece of shell in the bowl, which Victoria quickly fished out and threw away.

"You don't want to use the mixer?" Sophie asked.

"You mean a Kitchen-Aid mixer?" It hadn't even crossed Victoria's mind that Travis might have one.

Sophie nodded. "It's in the closet. We always use it for the cookies. So you don't really need two bowls."

Victoria laughed. "You're right. And that will make things much easier."

She got the mixer, which was bright red, and put it on the counter and they added the cold butter and sugar to the bowl, then turned the mixer on. Once it was creamed and fluffy, she poured in the eggs and the vanilla, then slowly added the dry ingredients which Sophie had mixed together first in the other bowl.

Once the dough looked right, Victoria had Sophie pour the bag of chips in and, after a few turns of the paddle, they were mixed in and ready to go.

They both scooped the dough into balls and placed them on a cookie sheet. Victoria slid the pan into the oven and began cleaning up their mess. Sophie helped by drying the dishes as Victoria washed them. Victoria was a little surprised by how much she was enjoying herself. Sophie was cute and mature for her age.

When they finished cleaning up, it was just about time to take the first batch of cookies out of the oven.

"They smell ready!" Sophie said excitedly. And Victoria had to agree. The kitchen smelled of sugar and vanilla and chocolate. She couldn't wait to try one.

"We have to let them cool for a few minutes. Let's get the next batch in the oven, and then we can try one."

Once they got the second tray in the oven, Victoria handed a warm cookie to Sophie and took one for herself. She poured two glasses of milk and they sat and enjoyed their cookies and milk and both went back for seconds.

When all the cookies were baked and the pan scrubbed clean, they went into the living room and Victoria smiled to herself. She couldn't believe she'd bothered to bring her laptop. There was no way she would be able to sit and write while Sophie played. Sophie talked to her constantly. She was full of questions. She wanted to know what Victoria did for work and if she was married.

"I'm not married. I don't have a boyfriend right now."

"My daddy doesn't have a girlfriend. You should marry him!"

Victoria laughed. Things were so simple to a four-year-old. "Your father and I are just friends. We've known each other since we went to school together."

"You went to school together? Here on Nantucket?"

"We did. Right here on Nantucket."

A minute later, as Victoria was about to click on the TV and find something for them to watch, Sophie jumped up and returned with a picture book. "Will you read this to me? It's my favorite book."

Victoria smiled. The book was *Fancy Nancy*, a popular series about a six-year-old girl that loved to dress up and be fancy.

"Sure, let's read it." She opened the book and turned to the first page. Sophie snuggled next to her on the sofa and Victoria began to read aloud.

*T*ravis found his father and Kay in the emergency room at Nantucket Hospital. His father had been triaged and was in a patient room wearing a hospital johnny and sitting on a bed. He had a bunch of stickers and wires on various parts of his body and looked grumpy as he sat waiting for the doctor.

Kay sat next to him in one of two chairs. Travis sat in the other and asked for an update.

"We don't know anything yet," his father said. "They stuck me with a needle and hooked me up to this contraption."

"How are you feeling, Dad?" Travis asked.

"I feel fine. I'm ready to go home."

"They took some blood and did an EKG," Kay explained.

"Do you have chest pain?" Travis asked.

"No pain. Just a little tired, that's all. That's probably why I passed out, I imagine. Just tired."

Travis had his doubts about that, but stayed quiet. They waited another forty-five minutes before the doctor came in.

"Hi, I'm Dr. Ambrose," he introduced himself. "Mr. Sturgess, can you tell me what brings you into the ER today?"

"Well, it wasn't my idea. I guess I passed out and when I woke up, my friend here strongly suggested we come in. So we did."

"Do you remember passing out? Any idea why that might have happened?"

"No. I went for a walk on the beach and next thing I knew, I was flat on my back. I think maybe I'm just tired."

"I see. Has anything like this happened before?"

Travis' father nodded. "A few weeks ago. But I was home and sitting on my bed. I thought I must have just laid down for a minute and drifted off, but I don't remember doing that. I didn't think much of it at the time."

"How long have you had your pacemaker?"

"About ten years, maybe?"

"Do you think it's his pacemaker?" Travis asked.

The doctor nodded. "I do. The batteries usually need to be replaced every eight to ten years or so. If you go longer than that, they can sometimes slow down and not do what they are supposed to. That could be why he fainted. All the bloodwork came back fine. I want you to call your regular doctor tomorrow and make an appointment to get a new battery."

"Is that a surgical procedure?" Travis asked.

"It is, but it's a minor one. He'll be home the same day and recovery is easy. Until then, take it easy. I wouldn't drive until you get that battery replaced."

"Dad, why don't you come stay with Sophie and me for a few days until you get all squared away?"

"Is that really necessary?" His father asked the doctor.

"I think you should," Kay said.

"If you were my father, I'd insist on you staying with me, just to be safe," the doctor said.

"Sophie will be thrilled to see you," Travis added.

"Alright then. Let's swing by the house and I'll pack a bag."

"*D*o you want to have another cookie?" Sophie asked sweetly. Victoria had just finished reading three *Fancy Nancy* books in a row and she'd thought Sophie might be getting tired. She glanced at the time and it was a quarter to seven. No wonder Sophie wanted something to eat.

"We should probably find something to have for dinner first. And then maybe have a cookie for dessert. What do you like to eat?" She figured Travis must have plenty of food in the house. Even though she wasn't much of a cook, she could pull something together.

"Can we have spaghetti?" Sophie asked.

"Maybe. Let's see what we have."

Victoria poked through the cupboards and found a jar of spaghetti sauce and plenty of pasta. That would work. She put a pot of water on to boil and once it was hot enough, she dumped in a whole box of spaghetti. She figured that Travis might be hungry when he got home and leftover pasta was easy to heat up.

Once the pasta was done, she drained it, then put the pasta back in the pot and dumped the jar of sauce in and gave it a good stir. She filled two bowls with pasta and found a bottle of grated parmesan cheese in the refrigerator. They sat down to eat and had only taken their first bites when the front door opened and Travis and his father walked in.

"Something smells good!" His father said as they walked in the kitchen.

"Did you cook?" Travis sounded surprised and grateful.

"Just heated up some pasta and sauce," Victoria said. "I cooked up a whole box so there's plenty more if you're hungry."

"We made cookies, too!" Sophie said. "And Victoria read me three *Fancy Nancy* books!"

Travis laughed. "Sounds like you had a good time. That was very nice of Victoria."

"Why is Grampy here?" Sophie asked.

"Good news. Grampy's going to stay with us for a few days." Travis glanced at his father. "Dad, do you want a bowl of spaghetti? I don't know about you, but I'm starving."

"I could eat."

Travis filled two bowls with pasta and joined Sophie and Victoria at the table.

"My dad needs to see his doctor on Monday. The ER doc thinks he needs a new battery in his pacemaker."

"Oh, that's good then. That's an easy thing to fix?" Victoria asked.

Travis nodded. "It should be a simple procedure. But until it's done, he's going to hang out here with us for a few days."

That seemed like a good idea. Travis' father didn't seem as keen on it, though.

"I told the doctor I didn't think it was anything serious. I could have stayed at home."

Travis shot him a look, and he sighed. "It's fine. I do appreciate your help. It will be nice to spend a few days with my Sophie girl."

"Grampy, will you read to me after dinner?"

"Of course I will."

"Good. We need to have cookies first, though," Sophie said.

"Most definitely. Those cookies do smell good."

When they finished eating, Victoria stood to go home and said her goodbyes. Sophie gave her a big hug, then ran and grabbed hold of her grandfather's hand and began pulling him into the living room to read to her.

Travis walked Victoria to the door and thanked her again.

"I really appreciate your time today. And for cooking. I owe you big time."

Victoria smiled. "You don't owe me anything. I'm just glad your dad will be okay. Sophie and I had fun today."

Travis's gaze softened. "You're good with kids."

Victoria stopped short. No one had ever said that about her before. "I don't actually have a lot of experience with kids. Sophie is just easy. I enjoyed hanging out with her."

"Well, I appreciate it more than you know. Thanks again."

"You're very welcome." Victoria went to step outside, then decided to update Travis on her online dating. "I took your advice, by the way, and went on my first online date last night."

Travis stopped short. "No kidding? How did it go?"

Victoria laughed. "It was awful. There was not a love connection. But I'm not giving up yet. I have another date lined up for the end of next week. How is it going with you? Did you have your second date yet?"

"Not yet. Michelle is traveling this week. We're supposed to go out this weekend for dinner, though. We'll see how it goes."

"I hope it goes well. Good night, Travis."

22

"I really don't know about this. Who is going to want to watch me on TikTok?" Lisa said. She and Marley were in Lisa's kitchen on a Saturday morning and Marley was helping her to make a few TikTok videos. Marley set up a tripod and had Lisa practice doing it herself, so she could make videos on her own without Marley holding the camera. The tripod was lightweight and Marley set it up on the kitchen island and aimed it at Lisa, so it would show what she was cooking on the stove.

They made a bunch of videos. Marley held the camera in some of them and followed Lisa around the inn as she gave a tour, showing prospective guests the property. They walked into several guest rooms, making sure to show the gorgeous water views. From there they went into the dining room, which was set for breakfast. The side table had a pretty roasted vegetable quiche, and there was a platter of cut fresh cantaloupe, honeydew melons and strawberries, as well as a bread basket with bagels and pastries. They walked down to the beach too and made sure to get a shot of the lighthouse in the distance and a ferry heading into Nantucket harbor.

"I'll edit this into shorter videos. People's attention spans are short so we'll have lots of short videos. I think we should do one of you making something that guests could easily make at home."

"Should I do the lobster quiche, do you think?"

Marley thought for a moment. "That's your signature dish and you sell it, so I think it's good to have a little mystery about that one. Let's do something simpler that they could easily make at home."

Lisa smiled. "How about the lazy-lobster casserole? It doesn't get much easier than that."

"That sounds good."

They went back into the kitchen and Lisa got all the ingredients out for the lobster dish. She tied an apron on and hesitated, looking to Marley for direction.

"Just talk as if you're telling me how to make it. Keep it casual and simple."

Lisa took a deep breath and smiled.

"This is one of the easiest and most delicious lobster dishes you'll ever have. The key is a pound of fresh, sweet lobster. You could also substitute any seafood really, scallops, shrimp, cod, or any combination." She leaned over and turned on the oven. "Set your oven at 350."

She dumped a bag of lobster tails onto a cutting board and lifted a giant chef's knife in the air. "First, cut your lobster into bite-sized chunks. Then put them in a nine by thirteen inch casserole dish." She chopped the lobster and added it to the dish.

"Now take one stick of butter." She cut it in half on the

cutting board. "Melt half of it." She put it in a bowl and then in the microwave for thirty seconds.

"While that's melting, go ahead and crush your Ritz crackers. You need one sleeve of them." She pulled a sleeve of crackers out of the box and laid it on the counter. "Now think of someone you're mad at and crush those crackers good." She grabbed a meat tenderizer and hit the crackers hard with it until she was satisfied that they were well crushed into crumbs. On her last whack, the paper wrapping split and a few cracker crumbs flew into the air and Lisa cracked up. "Whoops! Sometimes cooking gets messy. You just have to keep going."

Marley laughed. "That applies to more than just cooking."

"It does!" Lisa tried to focus and get back on track. "Now, pour your crumbs into a bowl and drizzle the butter over them. Stir and then sprinkle over the lobster. Then cut the rest of the butter into slices and spread them evenly over the top of the lobster. Slice a lemon in half and squeeze one half over the casserole. Add about two table-spoons of good sherry, just sprinkle it over. That's optional. I like a little hint of it though. Then pop it in the oven for fifteen minutes."

She slid the lobster into the oven and relaxed for a minute. Marley shut the recording off.

"Now we have to wait a bit. We can have lobster for lunch though, if that sounds good?" Lisa said.

"I was hoping you'd say that. I'll turn the camera back on when you take it out of the oven."

"You really think people might be interested in these videos?" Lisa asked.

Marley nodded. "Yes. People love food and travel videos on TikTok. You can do one every few days, just anything that comes to mind. Cooking or entertaining tips or short recipes. When the flowers start to bloom in the spring, basically anything people might want to see if they were thinking about taking a trip to Nantucket."

"We can get some good pictures when it snows, too. Nantucket is so pretty in the winter and maybe that might make more people want to visit then. Just to get away," Lisa said.

"I love the island in the winter. It's so peaceful," Marley said. "Oh and Christmas Stroll too... we can get loads of pictures then. The pictures don't all have to be at the inn. They can be things you might see or do on Nantucket."

"Like the Daffodil Festival's antique car parade in April?" Lisa said.

"Yes, absolutely. That's such a fun weekend to come here. It's like the unofficial start of the new season."

Lisa went to clear the dining room and put everything away. Marley helped her carry the leftover food into the kitchen. They finished up just as it was time to take the lobster casserole out of the oven. Lisa grabbed her oven mitts and Marley got the camera ready. Lisa set the casserole on the counter, smiled and addressed the camera. "This looks perfectly done. See how it's nice and golden brown on top?"

She used a serving spoon and ladled two generous portions onto plates for her and Marley's lunch. "Now let's see if it tastes as good as it looks." Lisa speared a chunk of lobster, put it in her mouth and smiled. "It's sooo good. You should really make this soon!"

"Well done!" Marley said and set the camera down. "I'll edit this all later and we can start uploading the videos." Lisa handed her a plate of lobster and Marley took a bite. "Yum. Maybe I'll make this for Mark soon."

"Rhett loves it. Especially when I do surf and turf and serve it with either a sirloin or filet."

"Oh, that is a great idea. That's what I'll do then."

23

*B*eth was about to shut things down at the office when one more call came in. She debated letting it go to voice mail as she didn't want to get stuck long on the phone. She was already going to have to rush to get to the Rose and Crown to meet the girls for drinks and trivia night. But it was still a minute before five. She picked up the phone. "Hodges Construction, how can I help you?"

"Is Chase in?" Beth didn't recognize the voice.

"He's at a site. This is Beth, I'm the office manager. Can I help or take a message for him?"

"Yeah, can you have him call Tony Mills? It's about a project he recently bid on for us. We went with those other guys, Cardoso, and it didn't work out."

"Oh, of course. I'll have Chase call you as soon as possible."

Beth immediately dialed Chase's cell. He picked up on the first ring.

"Hey there. Are you done for the day and heading out with the girls?"

"I am. You just got a call, though." She filled him in.

"That's interesting. Guess he found out cheaper isn't always better. I'll call him now. See you at home later. Love you."

Beth smiled. "Love you too. See you later."

Fifteen minutes later, Beth walked into the Rose and Crown and spotted Kristen, Taylor and Victoria at a big, round table in the corner. She hugged everyone hello, then sat next to Kristen.

"I talked to Abby earlier today, and she said she can't make it tonight," Beth said. "Natalie has a bad cold, and she doesn't want to leave her."

Kristen nodded. "Kate called me as I was driving over and said both of the twins are sick too, so she's staying home as well"

"Izzy and Mia should be here any minute, though," Beth said. She was looking forward to seeing them. They were sisters. Izzy ran a cute clothing store downtown, Nantucket Threads, and Mia was a wedding planner and did a lot of work with The Whitley Hotel. She had planned Kristen's wedding and Angela's too.

"Angela is on her way," Kristen said. "I haven't seen her in ages. She just got back from a trip to LA with Philippe."

"Did someone say my name?"

Beth looked up and saw Angela, followed by Izzy and Mia. They all settled at the table. Angela took the seat next to Beth.

"Kristen was just saying you just got back from LA. You lead such a glamorous life," Beth teased her.

Angela laughed. "So glamorous. Don't forget my day job —I was cleaning toilets and scrubbing floors all day. It was fun, though. But I'm glad to be home."

"You don't miss California at all?" Beth asked her. Angela had lived in San Francisco for years before moving to Nantucket, which was supposed to be a temporary thing, but then she met Philippe.

Angela shook her head. "Not one bit. I thought I would, but I never missed it at all."

"Mia! When did that happen?" Kristen squealed. The table grew silent, and all eyes went to Mia and her huge diamond engagement ring.

Mia looked a little embarrassed, but when they insisted, she held her hand up so the girls could all get a good look.

"Sam asked me last weekend. I thought we were just having dinner to celebrate my birthday. I didn't expect this at all. We went to Nautilus and had an awesome dinner and then when they brought out a crème brûlée for us to share, there was a bottle of champagne too, which I didn't remember us ordering. The server poured two glasses and then Sam got down on one knee and asked me to marry him. I said yes, of course. The whole restaurant clapped and cheered. It was crazy."

"Mia, that is so awesome," Beth said. They all loved her boyfriend, Sam, and figured that eventually they'd get engaged. Sam and Mia had met in a bereavement group. Sam was a widower and Mia's fiancé had died suddenly in a motorcycle accident a year prior. So neither of them wanted to jump into anything too quickly. Plus, Sam had two daughters and wanted to make sure whoever he dated would get along with his girls, too.

A server came to the table with menus and took their drink orders. Beth ordered a chardonnay and decided on a fish sandwich. A few of the others decided to split pizzas. After their drinks were delivered, the trivia host came by with a scoresheet, pencil, and answer pad.

"Beth should keep score," Kristen said. "You're the most organized."

Beth laughed. It was true, though. She had a knack for numbers and keeping things organized and usually ended up being the one in charge of keeping score when they played. "I'll do it. Unless someone else wants to?"

They laughed at the idea of it. A minute later, Taylor's boyfriend, Blake, stopped by the table. Taylor and Victoria usually played trivia with Blake and the rest of the team from the paper, as they came most weeks. It was rare that their group of girls actually managed to get out on the same night, and even rarer that it was on trivia night.

"You sure you girls don't want to play with us? We'd be unstoppable with all of this brain power," Blake teased.

"You're just scared we'll win," Taylor teased right back.

Blake laughed. "And you might be right about that. We'll see though. Just wanted to wish you good luck!" He chatted for another minute or two before heading back to his table.

"Looks like things are still going well with you and Blake?" Beth said.

Taylor smiled. "They really are. Especially now that I report to Joe."

That's right. Beth remembered that when Taylor started at the paper, she'd reported directly to Blake and even though there was definitely an attraction, they'd both been hesitant to act on it.

Blake's father had wisely suggested a restructuring that would let Blake focus more on the things he was good at and they could promote Joe, a reporter that had been with them for years, to a manager role. Both Taylor and Victoria reported to Joe now, and Taylor and Blake started officially dating soon after.

"Victoria, what's new with you?" Mia asked.

Victoria took a sip of her wine before answering. "Well, not much. But I have started doing some online dating."

"You are? How exciting!" Mia said. "One of my college friends met her husband that way. How is it going?"

"So far, I'm not all that impressed." She told them all about her first date and they agreed that Brad probably wasn't a catch.

"I had a date last night with a second guy and he was much more normal. Really nice, actually. It just felt like something was missing. Maybe I'm being too picky."

"I told her she should go out with him at least one more time," Taylor said. "Sometimes people don't wow you at first, but as you get to know them, they grow on you."

Victoria sighed. "That makes sense. I probably should. I just wish I was a little more excited about it."

Their food came soon after, and the conversation shifted. Kristen asked Izzy how her daughter was. Izzy had unexpectedly found herself pregnant right after she'd ended things with her boyfriend Rick, who'd grown increasingly angry about everything, as their relationship progressed. Izzy was very easy-going and made excuses for him at first. He'd lost several jobs due to his anger issues, and everything seemed to stress him out. Eventually, though, it reached a point where she couldn't make excuses any longer.

She'd ended things, and it was messy for a while as Rick tried to do better and attended an anger management course, and she debated giving him a second chance. But it was still too much and didn't feel right. She moved in with Mia, had her baby and, over time, found romance with Will, who had always been there for her as a friend.

"She's really great. She's my whole world, actually. Everything is so much better since she arrived. Will's great too, of course."

"Did you always know you wanted children?" Kristen asked.

Izzy nodded. "I did. But I wasn't in a hurry to have them. I never expected that I'd get pregnant when I did. The timing couldn't have been worse, really. But I always knew I would have kids one day."

"Are you and Tyler thinking about trying?" Beth asked. Kristen had never talked about kids before, but now that she was married, it made sense.

Kristen took a sip of her wine and hesitated a bit. "This might sound awful, but we have been talking about it, and I'm honestly not sure that I want kids. I've never pictured myself with children. Most people do, right? Tyler says he's fine either way. But I'm feeling kind of selfish about it."

"I don't think you should feel selfish at all," Victoria said. "It's a big decision. I've never thought much about it either. I've never babysat or was into dolls. I think if you know you don't want kids, then it's probably better if you don't have them."

"I agree with Victoria," Beth said. "One of my aunts never had children. She was always focused on her career and didn't want to have a child as a single mother because she saw how lonely her mother was after she divorced. She said the years flew by and suddenly it was too late, anyway. I do think she regrets it sometimes. She would have made a wonderful mother. But she did what felt right to her at the time. That's all you can do, really."

Kristen looked thoughtful. "That's what I wonder about, too. Will I regret this down the road when it's no longer an option? Right now, I don't think I will."

Beth smiled. "So then, it's the right decision for you."

"I guess it is," Kristen agreed.

Once they finished eating and their table was cleared, the trivia started and they focused on coming up with the right answers to the various questions. There were several categories. They all did well on the literature and movies categories and science and business, but sports and history were their weak spots.

"Blake was right on this. If we'd joined forces, we would probably win easily," Taylor said. "But we wouldn't be able to chat as easily. And we really don't do this often enough."

"Here's a food question and a bit of a mind teaser for you," the trivia host began. "What are the two things that you can never eat for breakfast?"

They all looked at each other with blank looks. Usually they did well on food questions.

"I have absolutely no idea on this one," Beth said.

The trivia host played a song after each question and sometimes the song itself had a clue to the answer in it. But this time, it didn't seem to. As the song neared the end, they still had no good suggestions. Until Angela laughed and picked up the pencil. She wrote an answer on the pad and held it up for them to see.

Beth smiled. Once she saw what Angela had written down it seemed so obvious. "I say we go all in and wager eight points."

Everyone nodded. Each round of trivia had four questions and they could bet eight, six, four or two points, but they could only use each number one time. So, the strategy was to use the low points on questions they weren't sure of.

Beth took the slip of paper. "I'll run it up."

She stood and walked over to the trivia host and waited in line to hand him her answer. He was set up with his speakers at a cocktail table next to the bar and while she waited, Beth heard two women chatting at the bar.

"So, how did your second date go? I can't believe you're dating Travis Sturgess. He's hot and his company is killing it. He has to be worth millions."

"Many millions, I'm sure. It's a public company, and the stock has doubled this year. The date went very well. We had a lovely dinner at Keepers. And we're going out again."

"Doesn't he have a kid, though? I thought I read that somewhere. You've always said you want nothing to do with kids?"

Beth turned slightly to get a glimpse of the woman who was speaking. She was pretty. One of the typical very blonde, very thin types one often saw on Nantucket. She looked like she walked out of a Lilly Pulitzer catalog with her pink and green print top and her pink cowboy boots. Her long hair was styled in a way that Beth envied a little—

it looked perfect, like she'd just left a salon. And her nails were elegant with a French manicure.

The woman laughed. "That was an issue, but there are ways around that. With his money, boarding school is an option or if he won't go for that, there's always a nanny. I certainly won't be playing mother to her."

"What if he's looking for someone that will?" Her friend asked.

"That can be managed. You know I always get what I want. That's why I do so well in sales."

"Did you want to give that to me?"

Beth snapped to attention when she realized the trivia host was talking to her.

"Sorry. Here you go. Thanks." She handed him the slip and walked back to the table.

As soon as she sat down, she told the others about the conversation she overheard. "Travis has become a friend. Chase just built his house and they know each other from growing up here. I feel like he should know what this woman is really like."

"Do you think Chase will tell him if you ask him to?" Mia asked.

"Chase has never been one to gossip," Kristen said.

"No. He hates that," Beth agreed. "Especially since he didn't hear them talking."

"Travis actually lives next to my parents' house. He told me about this girl. Is she blonde?" Victoria asked.

"Yes, obviously it's fake. No one is that blonde."

Victoria laughed. "That sounds like Michelle then. I think he's only gone on two dates. He'd told me he liked her enough to take her out again. They were going to dinner somewhere Saturday night. He didn't seem wildly enthusiastic, though."

"He's probably a little gun-shy after what he went through with Kacey," Beth said.

"Maybe I should say something?" Victoria suggested. "Although I think it might be better coming from Chase. Or maybe we just give it some time. Travis might figure out what she's up to on his own, and it will be a non-issue."

Beth nodded. "That sounds like a plan. I'll tell Chase and he can do what he wants. My guess is he'll agree with letting Travis discover for himself."

"His daughter Sophie is a sweet kid. If he doesn't figure it out, I may say something eventually," Victoria said.

They all grew quiet as the host announced the answer to the last question.

"So, what are the two things you can never have for breakfast?" He paused. "I thought this might be a really easy one, but only one team got it right. The two things you can never have for breakfast are lunch and dinner!"

24

"How are your sales today?" Marley called a few days later when Lisa was just finishing up the breakfast service. She and Rhett were done eating, and she'd been chatting with Kay before she left for her daily walk on the beach. Rhett was off to the restaurant, and Lisa had most of the leftovers put away.

"I haven't looked yet. I was late getting up today and had to get breakfast served. I'm sure they're similar to the day before, though. Why?"

"Why don't you check your email and recent sales numbers and then call me back?" There was a hint of mischief in Marley's tone that made Lisa curious.

"I'll call you in a few minutes."

Lisa opened up her laptop and checked her email first. There were close to twenty new reservations confirmed and at least that many inquiries—people with questions about the inn. She'd never had that many bookings in one day and never that many emails.

She clicked into her ecommerce order page next and

her jaw dropped. She had almost three hundred more orders than she usually had in a day. One of her emails was from the bakery off-island that made her quiches and processed orders. They asked her to call them as soon as possible.

Lisa called Marley first, and she answered on the first ring. "So, I'm dying to know... tell me."

"It was our best sales day ever....for the quiches and bookings for the inn. Is that from one of the TikTok videos? It didn't seem like the ones you posted were getting much attention. I didn't look today, though."

"I posted the video of you making the lobster casserole yesterday afternoon and it went a bit viral." Marley sounded excited.

"I don't understand, though. That video did so much better than the others? Why?"

"I think it's because you had that moment where you whacked the Ritz crackers and some of them got loose. You laughed and people liked what you said."

"What did I say?" Lisa couldn't even remember.

"You said 'Sometimes cooking gets messy. You just have to keep going.' And people loved it. You're getting stitched and that part, especially, is being repeated."

"Stitched? What does that mean?" Lisa wasn't up on all the things you could do with TikTok.

"It's when they clip some of your video into theirs and comment on it."

"Oh. That's a good thing, then?"

"That's a very good thing. The more people that comment on your video and share it this way, the better.

Yours really took off when this one chef that stitches someone different every day chose your video."

"What did he do with it? I hope he liked it."

"So, he stitches a food video and comments on it and says whether he'd eat the dish. He rated yours a 10 out of 10 and agreed that it's a good thing to get messy when you cook. That's how some of the best food is made. And he said he'd totally eat your lobster casserole. And lots of people are agreeing."

"So, they must have gone and looked at the other videos then, because sales of the quiche are through the roof. Three hundred more orders than normal. I have to return a call to the bakery actually. They're probably wondering what's going on. But there were lots of inquiries and new bookings for the inn too. Our busiest day ever."

"Behold the magic of TikTok! I am thrilled that it worked for you."

"It's pretty impressive. It's probably a fluke though, right? A sudden spike from this video. It won't continue, will it?"

"It's impossible to say. It won't continue for long without more videos. So, that's why it's important to keep making new content and uploading new videos regularly."

Lisa suddenly felt the pressure to get something exciting and new up. But she wasn't sure what would be as good.

"So, what do I do next? I don't really have any good ideas," she admitted.

"Hmmm. You usually make something for Sunday dinner, right? Even if it's just you and Rhett?"

"I was just going to make a big pot of meatballs and

sauce. That's so ordinary, though. I make it all the time. Rhett loves it, though."

"I've had your meatballs and they're awesome. Set the camera up and pretend I'm there and just film it all as you make it. Get a shot of Rhett tasting a meatball and maybe sipping a glass of red wine as you get ready to eat. Get a shot of the beach before it gets dark. Be sure to mention the inn every time. Then just upload your video and send it to me. I'll edit and put it up for you," Marley said.

"Okay. I can do that. You're sure meatballs aren't too boring?"

Marley laughed. "There's nothing boring about your meatballs. Send it to me when you're done—and remember to just have fun with it. Don't worry if you mess up. That's part of the charm."

"Okay, I'm ready to go home." Travis' father was sitting in the kitchen drinking a cup of coffee. His overnight bag was packed and sitting next to him. It wasn't even eight yet. Travis rubbed his eyes and poured himself a cup of coffee and joined his father at the table.

"How'd you sleep? Are you feeling okay?"

His father had his pacemaker updated the day before with new batteries. He'd wanted to go home afterward, but Travis had insisted he stay with them for one more night. He'd had anesthesia and though the risk was small, there was always the possibility of a complication.

"I slept fine. I'm as fit as a fiddle. And I appreciate all of your help, but I'm ready to go home. I want to be there when Kay takes her walk on the beach after breakfast."

Travis smiled. "Ah, so now I know why you're in a rush to get back."

"Well, she's not here much longer, you know."

Travis stood. "Let's go. I'll grab Sophie and we can head out."

"I'm right here, Daddy. Can we get blueberry muffins on the way home?" Sophie walked into the room. She was fully dressed except for her shoes.

"We'll see. Put your shoes on." Sophie loved the blueberry muffins at The Corner Table and it was on the way home.

Fifteen minutes later, they pulled up to his father's house. Travis carried his father's bag in, as he was supposed to be careful about lifting things until his incision healed. Sophie gave her grandfather a goodbye hug and ran out to the car, eager to get her muffins. Travis noticed that his father smelled good and recognized the scent. He must have splashed on a bit of Travis's cologne that he kept in the bathroom.

"So, you like Kay?" His father hadn't shown interest in any women since Travis's mother passed.

"She's good company. She won't be here much longer, so I just want to see her while I can."

Travis nodded. "Okay. Tell her I said hello. Are we still on for Scrabble tomorrow night?"

"Of course we are. See you here at six."

"I'm back. Stop by for coffee after your walk if you like."

Kay smiled at the text message from Walter. She was finishing her breakfast and planned to head to the beach for her morning walk.

She texted back. *"Be by in a bit."*

"You look happy about something," Lisa commented. It was just the two of them in the dining room. Rhett had already left for the day.

"Oh, it's nothing. Walter's back. He had his procedure yesterday. I'll stop by and see how he's doing."

Lisa smiled. "I'm glad you've gotten to know some people here. These weeks are going by fast. Have you thought about extending your trip? You could stay through the holidays or longer if you like."

"It's tempting," Kay admitted. "But I'm afraid if I stay through the holidays, I might never want to leave."

"Well, that's not such a bad thing. That's how many people end up moving here. I know you're excited about your Charleston trip though. I just wanted you to know you're always welcome here."

"Thank you. And I am looking forward to Charleston."

Kay said goodbye to Lisa and headed to the beach. It was a cooler day, and windy. She zipped her coat and pulled her soft cashmere hat out of her pocket and put it on. It was thin, but warm and cozy. Even though it was chilly, there were still plenty of people out walking. Kay said hello to some of them as she passed by and did her usual walk to the lighthouse. On the way back, when she reached Walter's house, she slowed and walked up his steps.

As soon as she reached the front door, he swung it open and invited her in.

"I saw you come up the beach," Walter said as he went into the kitchen to pour her a mug of coffee. They sat in their usual spot, in the two chairs facing the ocean. Kay took a sip of her coffee. It was strong and hot and she welcomed its warmth. By the time she'd reached Walter's house, she was feeling the cold. Once she took a few sips, though, she began to thaw.

Kay looked at Walter, who was sipping his coffee and staring out to sea.

"So, how are you feeling?" She asked.

He took another sip of his coffee. "Good. It's a simple procedure. Not like a real surgery. They just gave me a new battery. I'm good to go for another ten years at least."

"I'm glad to hear it. I missed stopping by here after my walks this past week," she admitted.

"I missed being here, too. But my son fussed about having me stay with him and Sophie till after the procedure. And the doctor agreed."

Kay laughed. "Well, they were right. I'm glad you're home now, though."

"So, what's new and exciting with you? What have you been up to while I've been gone?"

Kay thought for a moment. "Not too much. I'm still doing that needlepoint class and enjoying it. Nice group of women. I've become friends with one of them, Ginny. After we volunteered at the food pantry last week, she had me over to her place for lunch with a few of her friends. She lives over at Dover Falls. Have you ever been there?"

Walter thought for a moment. "That's the assisted living place?"

"Right. There's three levels actually depending what you need. Independent, assisted and memory care. Ginny is in the independent living. She likes it there."

"When Margery was sick, we thought about going to a place like that. But we decided against it. We both like being home and we were able to have nursing help come in when she needed it."

"If I lived here, I wouldn't want to move either," Kay said. "How could you leave this view?"

Walter smiled. "I never get sick of it."

26

"*Do you like lobster?*"

Victoria smiled at the text from Travis. It was almost four on Wednesday and she'd only had a small salad for lunch. Lobster sounded good.

"*Doesn't everyone?*" She texted back.

"*I'm picking up a few lobsters for dinner. Want to join us? I still owe you for helping me out and watching Sophie.*"

"*You don't owe me. But I do love lobster. What time?*"

"*Six. See you then.*"

Victoria was still smiling as she turned her attention back to her computer. Taylor walked by at that moment and raised her eyebrows.

"Did you decide you like him after all?"

"Like who?"

Taylor laughed. "Didn't you just have a second date with Richard last night? I assumed that's why you were smiling and texting."

"Oh. No. It wasn't Richard. The date was fine, but

there's just no love connection there. I'm not going out with him again."

"That's too bad. You're sure you don't want to give it at least one more try? Sometimes it takes a few dates."

Victoria shook her head. "I went out with him again against my better judgement. When you know, you know. He's a nice guy, though."

"Okay. So what has you all smiley?"

"It was just my neighbor, Travis. He picked up a few lobsters and invited me to come by for dinner.

"Hmmm, dinner? That sounds promising."

Victoria laughed. "It's not like that. He's just being neighborly. It's a thank you for watching Sophie."

"You guys used to date, though, right?"

"For about two seconds in high school. I didn't even recognize him at first." She didn't add that it was because he'd grown so much and looked so good.

"Is it because he's divorced with a kid?" Taylor asked.

Victoria nodded. "Partly. I never pictured myself as a stepmother to a young child. I've never been all that into kids, to be honest."

"Too bad. He seems like a good guy."

"Oh, he is! He's a great guy. But he's dating someone else anyway. That blonde girl we saw at the Rose and Crown."

"The one that said she doesn't like kids?"

"Oh, that's right. That won't last, but I'm sure he'll easily find someone else."

"Too bad. You'd probably have more luck if you put some pictures up. Have you reconsidered that?"

"Not yet. I'll keep it in mind, though. I still don't really feel ready to be that aggressive." Victoria laughed. "I'm hoping Mr. Right might just walk up to me when I'm out somewhere. That would be so much easier."

"Well, they do say that you meet people when you least expect it, when you aren't really looking. And that's how it happened with Blake. I never imagined I'd want to date my boss. You just never know."

Sophie opened the door when Victoria knocked at six sharp.

"Come in! We're having lobster. And I got a new *Fancy Nancy* book today. My Grampy got it for me. He read it to me, but maybe you'll read it to me too after dinner?" The words came out in an excited rush.

Victoria nodded. "Sure, we can do that. I bet it's a good one."

Sophie's face lit up. "It's soooo good." Her eye went to the paper bag that Victoria was holding. "What's that?"

"It's a bottle of wine, to go with dinner."

"Yuck!"

Travis chuckled as he walked out of the kitchen toward them. "The wine is not for you, young lady. Why don't you go and mix yourself a chocolate milk?"

Victoria handed him the bag. "I stopped at Bradford's Liquors on the way home and asked Peter what he'd suggest for lobster."

Travis pulled the bottle out of the bag. "Louis Jadot Pouilly Fuisse. I haven't had this before."

"He said it's like a chardonnay."

"Sounds good to me. Thank you. Are you ready for a glass?"

"I'd love one." Victoria followed Travis into the kitchen

and watched as he expertly opened the bottle and poured two glasses, and handed one to her.

She took a sip and looked around the kitchen. A big styrofoam box sat on the counter and the table was set for the three of them. Travis reached into the refrigerator and pulled out a carton of potato salad. He then turned his attention to a pot boiling on the stove.

"The corn should be just about ready." He turned the heat off, strained the pot over the sink and put the corn on a big platter and brought everything over to the table.

"Can I do anything to help?" Victoria offered.

"There's a lemon in the refrigerator, if you want to slice it up. I have butter melting in the microwave. We're just about ready." He opened the styrofoam container and pulled out three lobsters and put each on a plate. There were already bowls on the table for shells and lobster crackers and picks to get the meat out of the shells.

Victoria took a sip of the wine. It was good, cool and crisp and buttery. It reminded her of the chardonnays she usually drank, but it was a little smoother. She brought the cut lemon to the table, and they all sat and began to eat. Travis helped Sophie to crack her lobster and get the tail meat out. She wanted to do the claws herself though and though it took her longer, she managed to crack them and dig the meat out. Victoria squeezed the lemon into her small bowl of butter. The lobster was so sweet and delicious dunked into the melted butter.

"I introduced Sophie to lobster when we first moved here and she loved it," Travis said.

Victoria was impressed. Most young children she saw seemed to eat nothing but chicken fingers.

Like many children, though, Sophie didn't have a huge appetite. She managed to eat about half of her lobster before saying she was full and wanted to go watch TV.

Once she ran off to the sofa, Travis topped off their wine glasses. The lobster was so good that Victoria took her time with it, savoring every bite.

"So, what's new with you? How's the online dating going?" Travis asked.

Victoria made a face. "Not so great. I've gone on a few dates, but no sparks yet. What about you?"

"Okay. I've gone on a few dates with the girl I mentioned, Michelle. She's very pretty, has a great job, seems to totally have her life together. We're going out again this weekend, to a wine dinner at The Whitley."

"Oooh, that's fancy. You must really like her." Victoria took a sip of her wine, curious to hear his answer.

"She's nice enough. It was her idea to go to the wine thing. I honestly am not sure, though. It still feels like something is off, but I can't put my finger on what it is."

"How is she with kids? Has she met Sophie yet?"

Travis frowned. "Not yet. Michelle says she's fine with kids. But I don't want to introduce anyone to Sophie until I'm really sure how I feel about them."

"That makes sense."

"Victoria, are you done eating?" Sophie called out.

Victoria laughed. "Almost. I'll be over in a few minutes." She took another bite of lobster and sipped her wine.

"Let me guess, she already asked you to read to her?" Travis said.

"She did. The minute I walked in."

"Are you sure you don't mind?"

"No. She has a new *Fancy Nancy* after all. I want to see what happens, too."

Travis laughed. "You're good with her. No offense, but I never pictured you as being into kids."

Victoria was tempted to agree with him, but instead said, "She's easy to be around. You've done a good job with her."

He looked pleased to hear it. "Thank you. My father has been a huge help too. Moving back here was definitely the right decision. I didn't have any support on the West Coast. I could have hired a nanny, but that's not the same as family."

"No, it's not. I wasn't keen on moving back to Nantucket after living in Boston, but now that I'm here, I can't imagine moving again. I think I appreciate being around family more now that I'm older," she admitted.

After they finished eating, Travis cleaned up in the kitchen. Victoria offered to help, but Travis told her he could manage and she went to join Sophie on the living room sofa. Travis could hear Victoria reading softly as he worked in the kitchen. She read with enthusiasm, slowly and dramatically, and Sophie was delighted. She laughed several times as Victoria read. When Travis finished, he brought his glass of wine into the living room and sat in an adjacent overstuffed chair and listened as Victoria finished reading the story. Sophie was snuggled close to Victoria's side, with her head resting against Victoria's side. They looked cute together.

It was a side of Victoria that Travis hadn't seen before.

He remembered her as being very competitive and focused. Victoria had been the salutatorian in their class. He'd been the valedictorian. School had always come easily to him. Victoria had also been the class president and a varsity cheerleader and, of course, she'd dumped him for the star quarterback of the football team. Admittedly, Travis had been going through a nerdy phase in high school. He hadn't really come into his own until college when he had a growth spurt and grew to just over six feet tall freshman year.

The few weeks he'd dated Victoria, though, had been fun ones. He remembered her as always being up for an adventure, full of energy and in a good mood. And she loved ice cream. They'd spent several afternoons after school and on the weekend at the soda fountain counter at Nantucket Pharmacy. The pharmacy looked like it was straight out of the 1940's and he'd felt like he was starring in an old-fashioned rom com when he was there with Victoria. He'd loved the time they'd spent together and was totally crushed when she moved on to Todd. He knew she thought she was being considerate when she gave him the news. She'd stopped by his house and he was thrilled at the surprise visit and thought it meant that she was getting more serious about him until she'd dropped her bombshell.

"Travis, I really like you. But I have to be honest about something. I can't see you anymore because Todd has asked me to be his girlfriend. I hope we can still be friends?"

He'd been so stunned and deeply disappointed that he couldn't get any words out. He'd just nodded and watched miserably as she walked out of his life.

As he glanced at Victoria now, with his daughter by her side, something stirred inside him. Victoria had grown up, mellowed a little, and he liked seeing this side of her. Could he ever see her that way again? It was certainly tempting. But could he trust that she wouldn't break his heart again? That wasn't a risk he was ready to take just yet. He didn't even know if she'd be open to it. He hadn't gotten that kind of vibe from her at all.

Maybe they would be better off as friends. He wouldn't want to jeopardize that, especially as Sophie seemed to really like her. He needed to be careful with his love life because it didn't just impact him—his choices affected his daughter too and right now, she was his top priority.

27

"Are you still upset about Cardoso swooping in again?" Beth asked. She and Chase were home for the evening, sharing a pizza for supper. Chase had been quieter than usual, ever since getting a call late in the day to let him know he'd lost another bid to the Cardoso builders.

"No. I'm just tired. I am irritated, of course, and felt like warning the client off, but that didn't feel right."

"You mean letting them know about the job you just got after Cardoso underbid and then screwed it up?"

He nodded. "It's true, but I couldn't bring myself to go there."

"I have an idea. Why don't you just drop them an email tomorrow thanking them for the chance and to keep you in mind for future projects, or if anything changes on this one?" Beth suggested.

Chase smiled. "Oh, that might work. I'll do that." He leaned over and gave her a quick kiss. "I knew there was a reason I married you."

Beth laughed. "How is the new project going?"

"Good. It will keep us busy for a while and they already told me they are much happier with the work we are doing."

"Well, it won't surprise me if you end up getting this other job too. I doubt that it was a fluke with Cardoso."

"That's what I'm wondering about, too. So, I'm not going to worry about it. Maybe we'll end up with it after all. If not, there will be plenty of other projects."

"Speaking of projects. I'm itching to do another flip. I've been keeping an eye out for possible properties, and I think there may be something interesting coming up."

Chase looked intrigued. "Oh, what's that?"

"There's an estate auction coming up next week. It's a rundown small cottage. The owner was in a nursing home and the house sat empty for a number of years. It's a good location, but it's basically a tear down."

"So you're hoping the condition of the place might scare people away?"

Beth nodded. "Yes, unless another developer has interest, which is possible, we might not have a lot of competition for this."

"If we get it, I could try out a new design I've been playing with. It has a small footprint, about 1500 square feet, but it's a good use of the space. All one level, with a cathedral ceiling in the living area that opens into the kitchen. Two bedrooms and a bathroom behind the kitchen and on the opposite side, next to the living room is the primary bedroom and bathroom. Full basement that can be finished and big sliders that can open onto a deck.

We could do lots of big beams for a rustic contemporary cottage look."

Beth could see the house as Chase described it and she could picture how she'd want to decorate too, with lots of natural wood tones and soft sea colors in the bedrooms.

"I hope Cardoso doesn't show up to this one. I hear he's looking to do flips too," Chase said.

"Ugh. I hope not. But he might not be our only competition. We'll work out what we can do and just stick to our budget. If we get it, we get it," Beth said.

28

"What are you trying to do?" Rhett asked before taking a sip of the cabernet that Lisa had just poured for him. He was sitting at the kitchen island snacking on cheese and crackers while Lisa fiddled with putting her camera onto a tripod and aiming it at the stove.

"I'm making a TikTok," she explained. "Now be quiet for a minute. I have to film this."

She took a deep breath and smiled at the phone. "This is a simple recipe, but it's my husband Rhett's favorite meal, so we have it often." She went on to describe how she made the meatballs and sauce. "Mix a pound or so of ground beef in a big bowl with bread crumbs or leftover bread. I do a little of both. First, I soaked it in some milk, that helps to tenderize the meat. I add it along with one egg, some Italian seasoning and a little fresh parsley. Roll it into balls and bake in the oven for fifteen minutes or so." She put the tray of meatballs into the oven and turned the camera off.

Then a minute later she turned it on again and smiled big. "Okay, now that the meatballs are baking, let's make the sauce." She sliced an onion and minced two cloves of garlic. "Add a little olive oil into a big pot, heat it up to medium, then add your onion and garlic and cook for a few minutes." She turned the camera off again and glanced at Rhett, who was watching and looking amused.

"You seem so serious," he said. "But you're doing a great job. They'll love your meatballs."

Lisa took a few sips of her wine and tried to relax before turning the camera on again. "Okay, now we add a can of crushed tomatoes, and grate one small carrot in for a little natural sweetness. A generous shake of Italian seasoning and a pinch of salt and pepper and that's it. Stir and let it simmer."

She turned the camera off again and helped herself to some cheese and crackers. A few minutes later, it was time to add the meatballs to the sauce.

"And that's it! Once the meatballs are in the sauce, I like to give it about 45 minutes for the meatballs to cook through and the flavors to develop. Ten minutes before I'm ready to eat, I'll cook up the pasta."

Lisa joined Rhett at the island and chatted about their days until it was time to eat. Then she turned the camera on for one final video. She'd already cooked the pasta and put some onto two plates, then added sauce and meatballs.

"And now it's time to see how they came out." She handed a plate to Rhett and set one down for herself. "Rhett, do you want to take the first bite and let us know how I did?"

Rhett looked surprised but quickly recovered and picked up his fork and cut into the meatball, then took a bite. He gave Lisa a thumbs up. "Delicious, as usual."

Lisa laughed. "And there we have it. Meatballs and sauce from the Beach Plum Cove Inn on Nantucket. Be sure to go to my website for the full recipe and while you're there, maybe order one of my famous lobster quiches. Thanks for watching!"

She turned off the camera and flopped onto her stool. "Was that okay, do you think?"

Rhett looked up from his meatballs. "You did fine, honey. Will anyone actually watch this? I'm really not sure about TikTok."

"I don't know. I hope so. My earlier video did well and brought a lot of sales and bookings. But, this is pretty ordinary. I think most people know how to make meatballs and sauce."

"Not necessarily," Rhett said. "You might assume that because you love to cook and it comes easily to you. But a lot of people find it intimidating. Especially the younger ones. I overheard two of my waitresses talking about it recently. They're both in their twenties and neither one really knows how to cook. I don't think they teach it anymore in school."

"They don't," Lisa agreed. "The kids didn't have it. Not like when we were younger. Though I did not do well with the sewing portion."

Rhett chuckled. "Well, lucky for me, you excelled at the cooking part. So what happens with your video now?"

"I'll send it to Marley in the morning and then she'll

edit it and post it for me and then we wait and see if people like it. And then I have to come up with new ideas for videos. I thought I might take a break from the food and take a walk along the beach. Maybe I'll borrow Walter's metal detector and try my luck. That might be fun."

29

*T*ravis pulled his truck up to the valet station at the Whitley Hotel. A valet opened the passenger side door and helped Michelle out. Her heels were so high that Travis wondered how she managed to stay upright, but she looked beautiful. She was wearing a white sweater dress with some kind of fur around the edges and her hair was curled and looked really pretty. She seemed excited about the event.

Travis would have preferred a quiet dinner out some-where, but he did agree it was a good idea to do something different. He'd never been comfortable in a suit and tie and knew that he would be expected to wear one at an event at The Whitley. It was one of the island's most luxurious hotels, right on the ocean, and known for both impeccable service and exquisite food.

Travis handed his car keys to the valet and headed into the lobby with Michelle. The floors were marble, and the ceilings were high and the overall feeling was elegance and luxury. Michelle was a few steps ahead of him and seemed to know where she was going.

"The event is in the ballroom, it's at the end of this hall," she said.

There were at least a hundred or so people already gathered in the huge function room. Tuxedo-clad servers walked around offering a welcome glass of Prosecco.

"This is set up like a wedding," Michelle said. "So we need to look for our place cards with the table numbers on them." She led the way to a big table and searched until she saw their names and grabbed the cards. "We're at table seven."

When they reached table seven, Travis noticed that most of the seats were already filled with elegantly-dressed women and several men. Michelle seemed to know them all and introduced Travis to the others at their table. He nodded, as the names went in one ear and out the other. He was good at remembering people's faces, but usually needed to hear the names a few times for them to stick.

"I'm so glad you guys are here. This is going to be so fun!" a woman across the table said. She looked to be about Michelle's age and Travis was a little surprised that Michelle knew them all and they ended at the same table.

"Last year's event was so good, I didn't want to miss it," Michelle said. She turned to Travis. "Lindsay is on the committee for this event. She was in charge of table assignments."

That explained it. Travis nodded and took a sip of his wine. "It's a great fundraiser for the library," Michelle added.

He did like that the library was benefiting from the

event. Sophie loved the Nantucket library and his father liked to take her there for story hour. It was a worthy cause.

Once everyone was seated, the wine dinner began. Travis lost track of how many courses they had. Each was a small plate of food and most were accompanied by a different wine. Everything was delicious, but the sautéed local scallops in a brown butter sauce and the veal scallopini in a creamy marsala sauce were his favorites.

"Isn't this crème brûlée fabulous?" Michelle said as she dipped her spoon in for another bite.

It was pretty good. Travis was almost finished with his. The creamy vanilla custard topped with a sheet of broiled sugar that cracked like glass was one of his favorite desserts.

"I just got the most wonderful new nanny," Lindsay announced.

"Did your old one leave?" The woman next to her asked.

Lindsay smiled. "No, I still have Alicia, but now we have Phoebe, too. Having two nannies is the best thing ever. There's always someone available to help."

"How many children do you have?" Travis asked. He assumed she must have a huge family, to need two nannies.

"Oh, just one. But she's a handful."

That didn't compute for Travis. He glanced at Michelle and spoke softly. "What does Lindsay do for work?" He imagined she must have a high-stress job that required her to work long hours.

Michelle laughed. "Lindsay doesn't work. She's a stay-at-home mother. She does volunteer work, though. That keeps her very busy at times."

"I've been looking into boarding schools," Lindsay said. "Bement will take third-graders. It's an excellent junior boarding school. That's only a year away."

"Oh, that's great. I didn't realize they could go to boarding school at that age," Michelle said. The others all agreed that it was a wonderful thing. Travis looked around the table and felt like he was in an alternate world. Who would send such a small child off to boarding school? And be excited about the idea?

"Jeremy and I went to dinner last night to celebrate our fifth anniversary, and I floated the idea by him. He seemed a little surprised at first, but when I pointed out that we'll have so much more free time together, he agreed that it could be a very good thing," Lindsay said.

Michelle smiled and nodded in agreement. Travis realized that the child in question wasn't even Lindsay's. Michelle put her hand on his arm and looked into his eyes. "I'm so glad we did this. Isn't it fun? And I'm so happy you got to meet some of my friends."

He forced a smile. "The food was delicious." And it was the best part of the evening.

Later, when they said their goodbyes and were in the truck driving home, Travis was mostly quiet until he pulled into her driveway. He got out of the car and walked her to her front door. But instead of giving her a goodnight kiss, he asked a question.

"Your friend Lindsay, with the nannies and boarding school when her stepchild turns eight. What do you really think of that?"

Michelle hesitated, obviously picking up an edge in his tone.

"What do you mean?"

"I know you said you like kids, but what does that mean? Would you want nannies and boarding schools, too?"

"I think it could be helpful to have a nanny. I plan to keep working for a long time."

Travis smiled. "Well, I work from home, so I don't think I'd ever have a need for a nanny, especially with my father nearby. And I can't imagine sending Sophie off to boarding school at any age, let alone third grade."

"Boarding school can be a really good thing. The schools are excellent."

"I think that people that send young children to boarding school just don't want to have their kids around," Travis said.

Michelle opened her mouth and looked like she was going to protest, but instead smiled and changed the subject. "I had a really good time tonight." She waited a moment for him to kiss her and when he didn't move, she leaned in and kissed him lightly. "I hope I'll see you again soon."

Travis just nodded. "Good night, Michelle." He didn't think he would be seeing her again any time soon. Now he knew why something felt off with Michelle. She'd said that she liked kids, but how she reacted both with him and over dinner when she shared Lindsay's excitement showed him how she really felt. He and Sophie deserved better.

"*I* can't believe this is our last week already," Kay said. She was in her usual spot at the needle-point shop, sitting next to Ginny.

"It has gone by fast. I'm thinking about signing up for the next class that starts right after the New Year. Too bad you won't be here. I'll miss our chats," Ginny said.

Kay looked around the cozy room, filled with women chatting and working on their needlepoint projects. She'd enjoyed coming here each week and would miss it.

"I'll miss our chats, too. This has been fun. Maybe I'll get back over the summer for a visit."

"I hope you do. You should experience Nantucket at its busiest. It's a fun time to come, everything will be open. We'll have to go have lunch at Millie's. That's one of my favorite places."

"That sounds like fun. I look forward to it."

Kay tried to feel some enthusiasm for her Charleston trip. She'd been so excited about it for so long, but now that it was almost time to go, she couldn't seem to capture that same sense of excitement. Maybe once she was on her way and arrived there, she'd be more enthusiastic.

"It's too bad you can't stay longer. Nantucket is really magical at Christmas. You've heard of the stroll? Everything is open that weekend and it almost feels like summer crowds. It gets busier every year."

Kay smiled. "So, I hear. It sounds very Hallmark-like."

Ginny laughed. "Oh, it is. There are carolers and decorating contests and a Santa parade. It's very festive."

"Maybe I'll come back one year and experience it."

"I hope you do. Oh, if you ever decide you might want to move here at some point, you could put your name on the waiting list for Dover Falls. I waited for over a year, so it may be a while, but there are openings now and then in the independent living section, where I am. I don't know how long the waiting list is now, but it doesn't hurt to put your name in, just in case. It doesn't commit you to anything," Ginny said.

Kay was tempted to do that, call and put her name in. She liked the feel of Dover Falls. Ginny's unit was comfortable and had lots of light. She also liked that everything was taken care of there, no mowing or dealing with snow removal, and Ginny said the food was good. It would be nice to not have to worry about cooking when she didn't feel like it. Kay had always liked to cook, but cooking for one just wasn't the same.

"Thanks, I'll think about that." As tempted as she was, Kay couldn't help thinking she was being impulsive. She had a home in Arlington, after all. And she had a fun trip planned. She intended on enjoying herself in Charleston. Nantucket had just cast its spell on her. It wasn't real. She could always return in the summer and she decided that she would definitely do that, come for a week or two and play tourist.

On Saturday afternoon, Victoria decided to head downtown and do some writing at The Corner Table cafe. It was too cold out to sit outside on the porch and she found it hard to focus at home with her mother and father bustling around.

Plus, she loved the soup at The Corner Table. There were always special soups of the day that were delicious. She arrived a few minutes before two and was glad to see it wasn't too busy. She'd missed the lunch rush. She got herself a cup of chicken curry soup and a hot tea and set her laptop up at an empty table. As she ate, she read over the last few scenes she'd written and thought about what needed to happen next.

It didn't take long before she was lost in her story world. The plot had changed a bit since she started and she was having a lot of fun with it. Victoria was so intent on her work that she didn't see Travis walk in.

"Are you writing your book?" He asked.

She looked up and smiled. "Hi! Yes. It's too cold to sit

outside now, so I've started coming here on weekend afternoons."

"You're not distracted by people coming and going or talking around you?"

"Not usually. Unless they are really loud. It's all white noise. And the food is good here."

"It is. I was out running errands and thought I'd bring some brownies home for Sophie." He held a paper bag up and grinned. "Okay, me too. Yes, I have a sweet tooth."

"Good to know. I have a weakness for brownies too, anything chocolate, really."

"Want to split one? If you can take a little break from your writing. I got extra and I wouldn't mind having a few bites now."

"Sure." Victoria closed her laptop and stretched her wrists. "I was due for a break, anyway."

Travis sat across from her and opened the paper bag. He set down two napkins, one for each of them, and split a big fudge brownie and handed her half.

"Thank you." She took a bite and closed her eyes for a moment, savoring the chocolaty goodness. When she opened her eyes, Travis was looking at her curiously. "You really do like chocolate."

She laughed. "Love it. So what's new with you? How are things going with Michelle?"

"We went to a wine dinner at the Whitley hotel last night. It was very interesting. I learned a lot." Something in his tone made her curious.

"You learned something about wine? Was it delicious?"

"It was. The food and wine were great. But I learned more about Michelle." He told Victoria about the conversation at the restaurant with Lindsay and then at Michelle's front door. "I got the sense that Michelle would be fine with shipping Sophie off to boarding school like her friend Lindsay, would prefer it even."

"Well, that would never happen," Victoria said automatically. She couldn't imagine Travis ever allowing it.

"No, and no nannies either. If I'm there, what would I need a nanny for? Plus, I have my father if I ever need someone to watch her." He grinned. "Or my neighbors."

"You've done a good job with her. Sophie's mature for her age."

"Thanks. She's a good girl. So, what about you? Have you met anyone interesting yet?"

"Not really. No one I've been excited about. I'm focusing my energy on my book for now."

Travis took the last bite of his brownie. "What is this book about?"

Victoria hesitated. How to describe her book in a way that wouldn't make him wonder. As her story changed, the love interest was quite similar to Travis, a single father and owner of a tech company. It wasn't totally Travis, just inspired by him, but she didn't want him to recognize himself and wonder. Because it was just a story and she was inspired by lots of real-life people and situations. She decided to keep it vague.

"It's a romantic-comedy of sorts. About two people that try online dating and funny things happen before they realize they are meant for each other. I don't think you'd like it. It's not a guy's kind of book."

Travis laughed. "You never know. I can appreciate the

occasional romantic comedy. *When Harry Met Sally* is a classic."

"That's one of my favorites. I've seen it so many times," Victoria said.

"Well, I should probably let you get back to your writing." Travis stood.

On impulse, Victoria invited him to join them her at trivia that Wednesday. "We usually head to the Rose and Crown right after work and grab a bite to eat before trivia. It's a fun group. You'd like the people I work with."

"I like trivia. I used to play now and then at a pub in San Francisco. I'll see if my dad can watch Sophie for a few hours. That sounds like fun."

A half-hour later, Victoria typed "The End." She felt a thrill of accomplishment. She'd actually finished a book. She'd edited it over and over as she wrote, constantly going back and revising, so she didn't think it would need too much work. She planned to go through the entire book again, and both Taylor and Beth had volunteered to be early readers. She wanted their opinion as regular romance readers. And Kate had given her the name of the editor and proofreader that she used for her books. So once she heard back from Taylor and Beth and incorporated any changes they suggested, she would send it off to the editor.

Victoria was nervous, but excited too. If they both gave her book a thumbs up, she would then see about getting it published. She'd talked to Kate about that too, as she wasn't sure if she should try to go the traditional route and submit it to big publishers or publish it herself. After asking Kate what she'd done, Victoria decided to follow in her footsteps and publish it herself. She was anxious to get it out there and see what readers thought of it.

And she had another story idea brewing. Whenever she got stuck on what to do next in this story, the other idea whispered in her ear. Kate had warned her about that and told her how important it was to tell the voice to wait its turn and to finish the book she was working on. But she jotted lots of notes down, though, so she wouldn't forget and could dive right in when she was ready.

32

"I can't believe it's been two months already. You're sure we can't talk you into staying for Thanksgiving?" Lisa asked.

It was Sunday night and Kay was in Lisa's kitchen for a last supper before leaving Tuesday morning. Tomorrow night, Walter was taking her out to dinner. It was going to be their first time going out for a meal and Kay knew it was just a goodbye dinner. She was going to miss all of them so much. And that was why she didn't want to stay for Thanksgiving.

"If I stay, I'm afraid I might never want to leave," she said with a smile. "I want to get to Charleston and get settled and start exploring."

"Will you go out to eat somewhere then on Thanksgiving?" Lisa asked.

"I might. Or maybe I'll just get something to go and relax in my room. I'll play it by ear. I am looking forward to doing several walking tours of the historic district. And maybe renting a car and driving to Savannah one day. I've never been there."

"I've been to Savannah. Lots of history there too. Pretty town." Rhett took a sip of the cabernet Lisa poured for all of them. They were having steak for dinner and it smelled heavenly. Kay and Rhett watched Lisa as she aimed a camera at the oven and took some closeups of the steak as she pulled it out of the broiler.

Lisa smiled at the camera before speaking. "See how that gorgonzola crust is perfectly browned? That's how you know it's done. We'll let that rest while we make the sauce." She added red wine to a saucepan with butter, beef broth, garlic, shallots and thyme.

Once it was all plated, Lisa got a final shot, then turned the camera off and they all sat down to eat. Along with the steak, she served fluffy mashed potatoes and roasted asparagus.

"Lisa, this is insanely good. Tastes like it could be served at a restaurant," Kay said.

Lisa smiled, pleased with the compliment. "Thank you."

Rhett nodded in agreement. "It's excellent. Better than what I've had at many restaurants."

"How are the videos going with TikTok?" Kay asked. Lisa had explained when she first set up the cameras that she was making a video for social media.

"Surprisingly well. Not at first. But the past few videos, the ones of me doing the cooking demonstrations, have been really popular."

"They liked the meatball one?" Rhett asked.

"Yes! I wasn't sure if they would. Meatballs and sauce

are so common, but maybe that's why it was popular. Everyone likes it."

"And sales are still up for the quiches?" Rhett asked.

Lisa took a quick sip of her wine. "Yes. Not as high as when the video first hit, but overall, sales are quite a bit higher than they were."

"Rhett, do you do them for the restaurant, too?" Kay asked.

Rhett looked surprised by the question and shook his head. "No, never even crossed my mind. I guess it should, though. Seeing how well it's working for Lisa."

"Kay, that's a really good idea," Lisa said. "And I can't believe I didn't think of it either. I've been so focused on my own videos. But Rhett, maybe you could have some of the kids that work there make some videos. They are all on TikTok."

"I'll talk to them. We can video nightly specials, cocktails, and I bet they'll have some other ideas, too."

When they finished eating, Lisa poured coffee and put out a plate of lemon bars.

"This is a new recipe I was thinking of making for Thanksgiving. It's gluten free, and Abby's trying to avoid gluten now, so I wanted to have something sweet for her."

Kay took a bite. The bar had a shortbread crust and a sweet-tart lemon curd topping.

"What do you think?" Lisa asked.

"I love it. It doesn't taste gluten free either."

Rhett picked one up, ate it in a few bites, and reached for another. "These are very good."

"Good! I'm glad you both like them. Kay, take a couple

with you when you go. There's too many for just the two of us, and I'll be making another batch soon, anyway."

"I will. I definitely want to plan a vacation here this summer. I'm curious to experience the island in the height of tourist season," Kay said.

"Oh, good. Let me know when you are thinking of it and I'll save the room for you. We do sell out often in the summer. And of course, if you ever want to come back before then, you are always welcome."

Kay smiled. "Thank you. It really is such a lovely place. I hate to leave, but now I know I'll be back again."

33

*K*ay dressed in her nicest sweater for dinner with Walter. It was a soft, baby-blue cashmere crewneck, and she paired it with a string of creamy white pearls and charcoal gray dress pants. She didn't usually wear much makeup, but tonight she added a little rosy pink blush to her cheeks, a bit of mascara and a swipe of glossy deep pink lipstick.

She felt both excited for the night out but also sad as she was leaving first thing in the morning, on the six thirty ferry. That would get her home by noon. She then had to be at Logan Airport in Boston by three for her flight to Charleston. It was going to be a long day. She'd thought about flying the next morning instead, but she wanted to just get down there as soon as possible. And she wanted to keep busy so she wouldn't have time to dwell on missing Nantucket and her new friends.

Walter picked her up at six and they headed off to his favorite Italian restaurant, Fusaro's. The restaurant was busy, but the smiling hostess recognized Walter and gave him a welcome hug. "It's so good to see you. Your table is ready." She led them to a corner table set for two and set down two menus.

"It's been a long time since I've been out to dinner with anyone other than Travis and Sophie," Walter said. He glanced around the busy dining room and sighed. "I didn't realize how much I missed it. I think you'll like the food here."

The scent of garlic and rich tomato sauce wafted over as a server glided by, carrying a tray of food. Kay smiled. "If it tastes as good as it smells, I'm sure I will."

They decided to split a bottle of chianti and ordered an appetizer of fried calamari to share before their dinners. Kay was tempted by the veal marsala, which is what Walter ordered, but went with the parmigiana crusted haddock served with a crab risotto. She loved haddock, a local flaky white fish.

When their server returned to the table with the wine, she poured and waited for Walter to taste and approve. But he surprised Kay by glancing her way. "Kay can try it first. I trust her judgment."

Kay picked up the glass and took a small sip. The wine was medium-bodied, and juicy with hints of cherry. Kay wasn't an expert on wine, but she loved trying new ones, and this one was delicious. She nodded at Walter and the server.

"It's very good."

The server filled Walter's glass, and he lifted it in the air. "To your next adventure. And don't forget to come back and visit us."

Kay tapped her glass against his. "I won't. I already told Lisa to expect me for a few weeks next summer."

"Good. You can experience Nantucket at its craziest. I love it here in the summer, but I have to confess, this time of year is my favorite. I love the peace and quiet."

"And now you have your family here," Kay said.

Walter smiled. "It's been great having Travis and Sophie here. I loved having them living with me, but it's fine now that they've moved into their house. I still see them almost every day."

Their server returned and set down a plate of fried calamari, which was cut into rings. It was cooked perfectly, so the squid was still tender and the batter was light and crunchy with a flavorful sweet and spicy dipping sauce.

"How long will you be in Charleston?" Walter asked.

"I'm thinking two weeks. Then I'll head home to Arlington until the end of the year. I may plan a trip to Japan to see my son and his family in February or March. I haven't been for a few years and, well, I have time to do that now."

"I've never been to Japan. I've thought about doing some traveling too. I talked to Travis about maybe taking a family trip to Italy. Sophie can see what real Italian food is like." He laughed. "Who am I kidding? I've never been either and I've always thought it sounded like fun to eat my way around Italy."

"Italy is wonderful. I did a trip with my girlfriends earlier this year and one of our stops was Italy. We went to Naples and the Amalfi Coast and it was beautiful. I'd love to go back someday and spend more time. I'd love to see Florence and Venice and Rome. Oh, and Tuscany, too."

Walter laughed. "There's a lot to see, that's for sure."

Their meals were delicious, and the evening was just perfect, as they sipped wine and chatted. One thing Kay loved about Walter was that he was so easy to talk to. They never ran out of things to say and sometimes they almost finished each other's sentences. He made her laugh, and she was grateful to have met him.

They shared an order of cannoli for dessert. Kay took a bite of the creamy cheese filling and the crunchy cookie shell, that was like a very thin waffle. She felt full and happy and smiled at Walter.

"I'm so glad I met you. I feel like I've known you for so much longer. I will keep you posted about my travels and will knock on your door when I come back this summer."

His eyes met hers and he smiled wide. "Well, I certainly hope so. I've enjoyed your company, Kay. I have to admit, I'm going to miss our morning coffee chats."

Kay nodded. "I was thinking the same thing. These weeks have gone by so fast and I've had such a good time. I am looking forward to coming back."

"And I'm looking forward to seeing you again. You don't have to wait until summer, you know. You're welcome to visit anytime. Though it sounds like you're pretty busy with your travel plans."

"I like to keep busy," Kay said.

Walter insisted on paying the bill when it arrived and Kay thanked him. It didn't take long to drive home. Everything on Nantucket was within a fifteen-minute drive and this time of year there was no traffic anywhere. Walter pulled into the driveway at the inn and walked Kay to the front door.

"Thank you for a wonderful evening," Kay said.

"It was my pleasure. When you come back, we'll do it again." Walter pulled her in for a hug and gave her a quick kiss on her forehead. "Safe travels, Kay."

Her eyes suddenly felt a bit damp as she waved goodbye and stepped inside. Leaving Nantucket was going to be even harder than she'd realized.

Kay arrived home the next day just before eleven. The ferry ride back to Hyannis had a completely different feeling than her trip to the island. She'd been excited then, full of anticipation for a wonderful vacation. And she'd had exactly that and more. The ferry going home, so early in the morning, had been half-empty, and it was a gray, damp day, which mirrored her mood.

Her house was in a nice section of Arlington, but when she walked inside, she stopped short and looked around her living room and kitchen. It was a small, cozy house, but it just reminded her of Al and the fact that he was gone. Pictures of their life together were everywhere. And her closet was still full of his clothes. She hadn't been able to bring herself to get rid of them. She realized that she was finally ready to do that and it would be a project she could tackle when she got home from Charleston.

Kay made herself a peanut butter sandwich for lunch, as there was no other food in the house. She did a load of laundry and repacked her suitcase with clothing more appropriate for the warmer weather in Charleston. She'd talked to her friend Cathy the day before and she and her husband had just moved into their new home in Arizona. And her friend Judy was down in Florida. She called an Uber to take her to the airport and as she passed by the houses her friends used to live in, Kay realized that her life as she knew it in Arlington was going to be very different.

Once she checked her luggage at the airport and got herself a cup of coffee, Kay still had over an hour to wait before it was time to board her flight. She thought about what Ginny had suggested and opened her laptop to look up the number of Dover Falls. And before she could change her mind, she called to inquire about putting her name on their waiting list. She could sell her Arlington house and move into Dover Falls if they had an opening. The thought of it excited her as she waited for someone to answer.

They put her through to the sales department and a lovely woman named Ava explained that the units were very in demand and the current waiting time for something to open up could be a year or longer. Still, she told Kay all about the different units and Kay let her know she'd be interested in an independent living one, like Ginny's.

"Oh, you know Ginny? She's great. We do have a longer wait for the assisted living and memory care, so something could open up sooner, but it's usually at least six months to a year on average."

Kay put her name in anyway, but felt defeated when she hung up the phone. It had been an impulsive thing to do and clearly it wasn't meant to be. Nantucket was so expensive that she could never afford to buy a regular house there. So, she'd have to settle for the occasional vacation. And maybe she'd have to get involved more with volunteering or other activities in Arlington and meet some new people.

34

*V*ictoria spent all day Sunday and Monday night rereading her book and doing a final edit before sending it to Beth, Kate, and Taylor on Tuesday. Once she had their feedback, she planned to incorporate any suggestions they had before sending it off to Kate's editor. She was nervous but also excited to see what they thought of it. She told them to take as much time as they needed and didn't expect to have feedback for at least a week or two, maybe longer. She knew everyone was busy and sometimes she was too tired to read at night after working all day.

When Thursday came, Victoria found herself looking forward to trivia even more than usual. She'd told Taylor that Travis was going to join them and Taylor seemed surprised at first, but then grinned and said, "Blake will love that. The more the merrier."

At the end of the day, they all walked over to the Rose and Crown together—Victoria, Taylor, Blake, Joe and Emily from sales. Blake spotted the table they usually liked to sit at and headed towards it. It was a big round table that could seat eight easily. As soon as they sat, Victoria saw Travis walk in and waved him over. He sat next to her, and she introduced him to everyone. Beth and Chase arrived a moment later and took the last two seats.

When their server returned with their drinks, they put their order in. Everyone was in the mood for pizza, so they got four different ones. As soon as the server walked away, Beth turned to Victoria. "I finished your book last night, and I loved it! I have a few minor suggestions. I will email you when I get home tonight, but I really thought it was great. I'm excited for you!"

Victoria looked at her in surprise. "Thank you. I can't believe you read it already."

Taylor grinned. "I told her the same thing when I got in this morning. I loved it too."

And Taylor had emailed her feedback as well. Victoria looked it over that morning and Taylor had caught a few inconsistencies-like using the wrong name—and she had a great suggestion for the one chapter that Victoria felt needed something more.

"So, what happens now? Is anyone else reading it?" Beth asked.

"Kate has it. Once I hear from her, I'll tweak it with all of your suggestions. Then it will go to her editor."

"Do you have anyone lined up to make you a cover?" Taylor asked.

"I thought I might give it a try myself. I've been researching this online and they advise against it—unless you have a good eye for design and know how to use Photoshop. I've used it for years, so I figured I would see if I can match the idea in my head. If not, then I'll find someone to help."

"Do you have any ideas for what you want for it?" Beth asked.

"The illustrated cartoon look is really popular for romantic comedies. I thought I might do something like that with a bright pink background and lots of pale yellow and blue flowers. I want it to be really pretty," Victoria said.

Beth and Taylor both nodded. "Pretty is good," Taylor said.

"Maybe I should read your book. Let me know when it's published," Travis said.

Beth and Taylor exchanged glances while Victoria hesitated. Finally she said, "Okay, I'll let you know, but I'm not sure it's your type of book."

Travis laughed. "Maybe not, but I still want to support you."

Victoria caught Beth and Taylor glancing their way again and reached for her glass of chardonnay. Taylor had mentioned it this morning too, after telling her how much she liked the book.

"It's obvious that you like him. Why not just give it a chance?" she'd said.

Victoria had quickly changed the subject, but she didn't feel like protesting anymore. She'd been thinking about it all day. She liked Sophie. Maybe her checklist of the perfect man needed an update.

One advantage of dating someone who had a child already—at least they knew what to do. And Travis was a good father. Maybe Victoria had made the wrong decision when she dumped Travis in high school, and this could be a second chance for them.

Their pizzas came and soon after, and it was time to focus on trivia. Their team rarely won, but with the bigger group, they were in the running from the beginning. They had a good mix of people that were strong in different areas. Travis knew a few tech and business questions that stumped the rest of them. And Chase and Beth had some real estate and building questions that they might not have gotten right otherwise.

When the final question came, they were in first place, but many times they'd seen teams come from behind on the last question and those who were in the lead lose everything. So they didn't take it for granted.

The trivia host announced the topic of the last question, the TV show *Seinfeld*.

Travis looked excited, but Blake reminded everyone that there were nine seasons of *Seinfeld* and each season had twenty-four episodes.

"I always think I'll know the answer on this because I loved the show and I always miss it," he said.

"There are a lot of us, though," Taylor said. "Odds are that someone might know it."

"Okay, let's go for it. We'll reserve one point just in case," Blake said.

A few minutes later, once all the wagers were in, the host asked the final question.

"What does George order from the Soup Nazi?"

"Oh, that was one of my favorite episodes!" Victoria said. "There was a soup shop near the paper in Boston that opened after that episode. They had the best soup." She laughed in frustration. "I have absolutely no idea what kind of soup George had, though. Jambalaya comes to mind, but I'm not sure."

"I think jambalaya is what Kramer used to order," Taylor said.

Everyone seemed stumped.

"And this is why I hate *Seinfeld* questions. They seem so simple, but I never know them," Blake said.

But then Chase, who had been quiet most of the night, suddenly smiled. "I think George ordered turkey chili. It just came to me."

"How sure are you?" Blake asked. They had about thirty seconds to turn their answer in and no other suggestions.

Chase shrugged. "I'm not 100% sure, but it feels right."

Blake nodded. "Okay, good enough for me." He jotted the answer down, then went to turn it in.

A few minutes later, the trivia host announced the final standings and the answer to the last question.

"So, only two teams got this one right. A lot of you put jambalaya, but the correct answer was turkey chili. Which puts the Nantucket News team in first place and the winners of a $25 gift certificate."

They all high-fived each other, and Blake handed Taylor the gift card when it was given to them. "Do you mind holding on to this? We'll put it toward the bill next time we play."

"How often do you all play?" Travis asked Victoria.

"Just about every week. You're welcome to join us anytime."

"Yeah, please come again. We need all the brainpower we can get," Blake said, and laughed.

After they settled the bill, they all walked out together and Travis asked Victoria where she was parked. She told him, and he nodded. "I'm heading in that direction, too. I'll walk you to your car."

It wasn't a long walk, and Victoria always felt safe on Nantucket, but it was nice to have his company as they walked.

When they reached her car, she decided to step out of her comfort zone a little. "Have you been to The Gaslight lately?"

"The Gaslight? No, I haven't been there ever, actually. Is it good?"

She smiled. "I like it. It's right downtown and has a fun menu and they usually have live music on the weekends. Maybe we could go sometime, if you want to check it out?"

Travis looked a little surprised, but he also seemed pleased by the suggestion. "How about Saturday night? I'm sure my father wouldn't mind watching Sophie again."

"Perfect. I'm glad you came out with us tonight. This was fun." Victoria opened her car door and looked back at Travis. He was still smiling.

"It was a good time. Let's plan on Saturday. I'll swing by around six thirty, if that works?"

"That works for me."

35

It was almost seven by the time Kay arrived at the Airbnb she'd booked in Charleston. She was staying in a huge old home in the historic district. The house was pale pink, with side porches on the first and second levels. The house had been divided into six units and Kay was on the first floor. There was a digital keypad on the door and Kay punched in the code she'd been emailed and breathed a sigh of relief when the door made a whirring sound and then opened.

She stepped inside, looked around, and smiled. It looked even nicer than the pictures she'd seen on the website. There was a small kitchen with a stove, microwave, and refrigerator, and there was also a fancy Nespresso coffee machine and a bag of mini-bagels. Inside the refrigerator there was a bowl of cream cheese and jam packets for the bagels and a half-dozen waters. On the table, there was a map of the area that was small enough to fit into her purse. It would come in handy the next day when she set out for her morning walk.

From the kitchen, she stepped into a living room area where there was a comfy sofa, coffee table and a big screen TV. That room opened into the bedroom, which had a non-working fireplace that was glowing merrily from tiny white lights that were wrapped around several birch logs. It was a soft, pretty look and made the room feel homey. The bed was queen-sized and was covered with a fluffy white comforter and plenty of matching pillows.

The bathroom was just off the bedroom and was small but elegant, with gray subway-tile, white cabinets and glass doors. She flopped on the bed and closed her eyes. It was very comfortable, and it was tempting to crawl right in and go to sleep after the long day of traveling, but it was a bit too early for that.

Kay headed back to the kitchen and saw something she'd missed at first glance. There was a bottle of red wine behind the bag of bagels, and a little note from the host wishing her a relaxing stay. She decided to pour herself a small glass of wine and read for a bit after she unpacked her suitcase.

The next day, she woke a little before seven. Sunlight streamed through the window, and it looked like it was going to be a beautiful day. After a quick shower, she helped herself to a few mini-bagels with cream cheese and a cup of coffee. And then she set off exploring.

Kay kept as busy as possible for the rest of the week. She walked all over the historic district, joined several walking tours, went to various museums, and had delicious southern food at many of the area restaurants. She loved shrimp and tried shrimp and grits at least once a day somewhere for either lunch or dinner. Her favorite places for it were at the waterfront restaurant, Fleet's Landing and at Rita's in Folly Beach. She took an Uber there one afternoon as it was only about ten miles from downtown Charleston and she was curious to see the beach. It was a pretty spot, and she spent all afternoon walking around and relaxing on the beach before catching another Uber back to her Airbnb.

She'd been happily surprised to get a text message from Walter on her third day.

"How's Charleston treating you? Seen any good sights yet?"

The text had come at just the right moment, when she was feeling a little down and missing Walter and everyone else she'd grown fond of on Nantucket. Since then, she'd been texting him every day or so, sending pictures of the places she visited and sharing any interesting tidbits of history. Charleston was full of it.

"Did you know Charleston had the first golf club in the country?" She asked him.

"No kidding? Maybe when you come back this summer, I'll give you a golf lesson, if you're interested?"

"That sounds fun!"

She knew Walter loved to play golf. She'd never had the desire to play before, but now that he'd offered to teach her, she found herself looking forward to it.

Thanksgiving morning, as she sat in her tiny kitchen, sipping a frothy cup of coffee, Kay wondered if she should have stayed for the holiday on Nantucket after all. The day stretched out, long and empty, and she wasn't sure what to do with herself. She went for a long walk all around the neighborhood and considered her options.

She decided to head out early to Poogan's Porch, which

was a restaurant she hadn't tried yet, and it was an easy walk to Queen Street. She got there when they opened at eleven thirty and asked if they had room for a solo diner. It wouldn't have surprised her if they were totally booked and couldn't accommodate her.

The hostess took a look at her reservations book and then glanced at the bar. "If you don't mind sitting at the bar, we'd be happy to have you. All of our tables are fully booked."

Kay smiled. "The bar is perfect. Thanks ever so much." The hostess walked her to the bar and handed her a menu. Kay sat and within a few minutes, another woman sat next to her and the rest of the bar filled up soon after. Kay ordered a mimosa and sipped it while she looked over the Thanksgiving prix fixe menu. There were so many options that sounded delicious, including the traditional turkey dinner.

She went with pimento cheese fritters to start, followed by her favorite Charleston dish, shrimp and grits, and for dessert, pumpkin cheesecake with a ginger toffee sauce. It was all scrumptious, and Kay enjoyed the hustle and bustle of the busy restaurant. The bartender was a character. He made her laugh and the woman next to her turned out to be good company. Her name was Alice.

Like Kay, she was a widow and usually hosted Thanksgiving, but this year her son broke his leg and couldn't travel and her other son was in Europe with his wife's family this year. Her son with the broken leg tried to get her to fly up to Maine to be with his family for the holiday, but the thought of battling the crowds exhausted her.

"I told him I'll see him in a few weeks for Christmas.

I'm going up there for two weeks anyway, so it seems silly to fly up for one day. I'm perfectly content relaxing at home. But I thought it would be nice to treat myself to a nice dinner out."

"I'm glad I decided to come out. This is really wonderful," Kay said.

"How long are you visiting?" Alice asked.

"Through the end of next week. Do you have any other ideas for things I should be sure to see or do?" Kay told her what she'd done already.

Alice looked thoughtful. "I was going to do a food tour with my son and his wife next week. It's a historic walking tour followed by a cooking demonstration and a food and wine tasting. I'd still like to go. Would you have any interest in joining me?"

"I would love to join you. That sounds wonderful."

Soon after she arrived back at her Airbnb, Kay received a text message from Walter with a group photo of him, Travis, and Sophie in Travis's kitchen. They were standing around a freshly-carved roasted turkey.

"Happy Thanksgiving Kay, from all of us."

"Thank you, same to you!" Kay sent him a picture of her dinner that she'd taken. Walter texted back a moment later.

"What no turkey? That's shrimp and grits, right? Looks pretty darn good."

It was delicious. But as she looked at the picture of Walter and his family, she felt a pang of regret once again, that she didn't stay on Nantucket for the holiday.

*K*ate got back to Victoria the next day with her feedback, and it was also positive. She had a few good suggestions as well, for areas that Victoria could tweak and expand a little to deepen the conflict. Her suggestions were really good and Victoria spent that Friday night and all day Saturday making the edits. She planned to go through it again the next day and once she was satisfied, she would email it to Kate's editor.

She finished up around five and jumped in the shower to get ready to go out with Travis. She felt excited and a little nervous. She wondered if Travis thought of it as a date? She hoped so, but she wasn't sure if he still thought of her as just a friend.

She took her time getting dressed and tried on several options before settling on her favorite jeans—the material was a dark blue and the fit was soft and flattering. It was cold out, so she went with a pretty rose-pink hand-knit sweater. She blew her hair straight, then curled the ends just slightly. And she wore a bit more makeup than usual, adding eyeliner and some brown and gold eye shadows. She chose a glossy peach-pink lipstick and searched around for her chocolate-brown cowboy boots.

At six-thirty sharp, Travis knocked at the door. He said hello to her parents and her mother couldn't have looked more thrilled that they were going out on a Saturday night.

"Have fun, you two!" she called after them.

Victoria laughed as they stepped outside. "My mother loves you."

"Your mother has good taste."

Travis drove, and they arrived at The Gaslight, which was downtown, in about fifteen minutes.

The restaurant was busy, but they were seated right away. The entertainment started in an hour and it was a blues band.

"Are you a blues fan?" Travis asked as he opened his menu.

"I couldn't tell you the name of any blues bands, but I do like the music."

"There's only one I can think of-The James Montgomery Band-I saw them play in Plymouth at Memorial Hall last year when I met up with some college friends."

Victoria ordered a glass of chardonnay and Travis got a Shark Tracker draft beer from Cisco Brewery, a local beer maker. They decided to share an order of pork dumplings and the tuna tostada as an appetizer and both ordered the caramelized miso salmon for their entrée.

Their conversation was easy as they ate. Victoria had worried that it might be a little awkward to make the shift from being friendly neighbors to dating, but it was like nothing had changed. Except that she noticed Travis seemed to be smiling more, and she guessed that she probably was too. There was a buzz in the air, a sense of anticipation that she hadn't felt in a very long time.

The food was delicious and when they finished, the band began to play. They stayed to listen to their first set. The band was good and the music fit her mood. They settled into a comfortable silence and enjoyed the music. After the set ended, the band took a break and said they'd be back in twenty minutes.

"Do you want to stay for the next set?" Travis asked.

Victoria wasn't ready to go home yet. "Yes, they're really good."

"I'm thinking about getting a coffee drink, maybe a Spanish coffee."

"That sounds like a dessert. I'll do the same."

A few minutes later, their server set down two glass mugs filled with coffee, rum, Grand Marnier and Kahlua. The rim of the glass was coated with caramelized brown sugar and a cloud of freshly-whipped cream sat on top. It really was like a dessert.

"How's your dad doing since you and Sophie moved out?" Victoria wondered if he missed having the company. As much as she was enjoying staying with her parents, she also thought it might be time to get her own place.

"He's good. I tried to get him to move with us, but he's not ready yet. He loves his house and I don't blame him. We still see him all the time, and I bet he enjoys the peace and quiet when we're not there."

"I think it might be time for me to find an apartment downtown. I'm getting a little too comfortable at my parents' place," she admitted.

Travis laughed. "I'm sure they've loved having you around, too."

The music started up again, and they sipped their coffees as they listened to the last set. When they finished, Victoria had to fight off a yawn. The day had caught up to her.

"Are you ready to head home?" Travis asked. She nodded. He insisted on paying.

"I'll treat next time," she said.

"And I'll let you. How about Thurday night at my father's? You can bring a bottle of wine, we'll supply the pizza. It's Scrabble night."

"Scrabble night? I haven't played that in years. You guys will crush me," she teased.

"Somehow I doubt that. I think I remember you as being just a tad competitive."

Victoria laughed. He was right about that.

"We could use a fourth, now that Kay is gone. I think my father really misses her. Though he says they're just friends. She was staying at the inn next door for a few months."

"Do you think your father will ever date again?" Victoria wondered aloud.

"I don't know. He was certainly pushing me to get out there, but when I asked if he wanted to try online dating, he seemed horrified. I think maybe if Kay was local, something may have developed. But it was just a long vacation for her."

"I'll play Scrabble with you. That sounds fun."

Travis grinned. "Sophie will be thrilled."

They headed home and Travis walked her to her door.

Victoria felt a rush of anticipation as Travis leaned in and smiled. "I had a really good time tonight," he said.

"I did too. Thank you."

Travis hesitated a moment, then pulled her in for a kiss. It was a quick peck, over almost before it began, but she'd liked the feel of his lips on hers.

"See you on Thursday," he said.

On Thanksgiving morning, a little before eleven, Lisa opened the box of Boston Coffee Cake and set it in the middle of the kitchen table. It was a tradition in their family on both Thanksgiving and Christmas morning to start the day with the coffee cake her family and friends loved—a moist yellow cake, filled with cinnamon and topped with streusel and walnuts. Lisa also set out a pitcher of freshly-squeezed orange juice and opened a bottle of Prosecco for mimosas.

By eleven thirty, everyone had arrived—all of her children and their spouses, as well as a few friends, Paige and Peter, and Marley and Mark. Everyone helped themselves to coffee cake and mimosas. Soon after, Lisa set out a charcuterie tray full of assorted cheeses, relishes and meats as well as a few other appetizers that had been requested—bacon-wrapped scallops and Chinese water chestnuts and mushrooms stuffed with spinach, sausage and three cheeses.

Lisa had done most of the prep work the night before.

Rhett had helped by peeling and chopping the butternut squash, while Lisa did the potatoes. She also made the stuffing—her grandmother's traditional sausage and bread stuffing—it was Lisa's favorite thing. She almost could skip the turkey and just eat the side dishes. Kristen and Tyler came early as Kristen liked to make the sweet potato casserole that was topped with brown sugar, butter, and marshmallows.

Rhett also helped with the turkey. He smothered it with a mix of olive oil and Portuguese hot pepper sauce. Lisa had been alarmed the first time he did it, but he'd told her to trust him. And he was right. The hot sauce on the outside of the turkey didn't make it too spicy, it just added some nice flavor.

Football played on the living room television and had most of the guys' attention while the women were gathered in the kitchen, chatting and snacking.

Abby's young daughter, Natalie, wanted to help Lisa cook, so she tried to think of a good task to give her. "Natalie, why don't you use this big spoon and push the cranberry sauce into this bowl?" She handed her granddaughter the can of cranberry sauce and showed her what to do. And that kept her busy for a bit.

By two, everything was ready, and the girls helped Lisa carry all the food to the kitchen island. Rhett carved the turkey and everyone helped themselves buffet style and brought their plates into the dining room.

Conversation was lively around the table as they ate. Paige and Marley had become good friends and they often double-dated, so now their boyfriends were friendly, too.

"What are your kids doing for Thanksgiving, Marley?" Lisa asked.

"They're going to Frank's house. His new girlfriend loves to cook, and she's our age. I think this one might last." She grinned. "The kids are coming here for Christmas, and I can't wait."

"How is Kay doing?" Paige asked. "Have you heard from her?"

Lisa had just received an email from Kay the day before. "It sounds like she is doing well. She said she's been doing a lot of tours and sight-seeing."

"What is she doing today?" Marley asked.

"She wasn't sure. She said she might get takeout, or if she was feeling really brave, she might go out to a restaurant," Lisa said.

"I hate to think of her being alone today. I hope she is doing something fun," Marley said.

"I do too. I tried to get her to stay, but she thought it might be harder to leave if she did. I think she really liked it here."

"That's how it was with me, too. I thought I was just coming for a few months. I never planned to stay longer than that," Marley said.

"Angela too," Kate said. "She was just on Nantucket temporarily until she could fix up and sell her grandmother's cottage. She fell in love with Nantucket... and Philippe."

"And I certainly didn't plan to stay at the inn as long as I did," Rhett said.

Lisa laughed. "You still haven't left!"

"Yep. You're stuck with me now." Rhett winked at her,

and Lisa felt a familiar warmth and sense of contentment. She couldn't imagine her life without Rhett by her side.

"Kate, how's your new book coming along?" Kristen asked.

"Slow. I'm at the beginning when I am not sure where the story is going. I think it should pick up soon though, hopefully."

"Did you get a chance to read Victoria's book yet?" Beth asked. "I ended up reading it in one night. I thought it was really good."

"I did. It took me a few nights to finish because I couldn't squeeze the time in. These past two weeks have been crazy with the kids being sick. But I loved it. I think she's already worked on our suggestions and sent it off to my editor."

"Does she know what to do after that? Can you help point her in the right direction?" Lisa asked.

"I definitely will. I think she's working on some cover ideas now. I can give her some marketing tips, too."

Marley looked intrigued at the mention of marketing. "Do you know if she's on TikTok? If not, she should be. Feel free to have her give me a call. I'm happy to help give her some other marketing suggestions too."

"Thanks. I will." Kate looked thoughtful. "I'm not on TikTok. Do you think I should be? Would it make a difference for the kind of books I write? They're not romance."

Marley thought for a moment. "I've read your books and I think it might help. If you can put together a short video that is like a teaser for the book, like a mini-movie trailer."

"That sounds like a great idea. But honestly, I wouldn't

know where to begin to do it. Is that something you could help me with? Could I hire you to make a trailer and put it on TikTok?"

Marley nodded. "Of course. Call me next week and we'll set up a time to meet and make a plan."

"Chase, how's everything going with your business?" Rhett asked.

Chase looked up from his mashed potatoes. "It always slows down a little this time of year, but it's better now than it was. We got a project back that we thought we'd lost to someone that put in a crazy low bid."

"And that same builder almost got a house we were bidding on last week at an auction. But they dropped out, and we got it," Beth said proudly.

"You didn't overpay for it, I hope?" Lisa asked. She knew how easy it could be to get caught up in auction fever. But she also knew it was unlikely, as Beth was very careful when it came to money.

"Oh, no, not at all. We didn't reach our ceiling bid. So we were pleased about that. They are new to the island and tend to underbid on projects to get the work. But they don't know the market as well as we do."

"Well, congratulations. I'm happy for you both," Lisa said.

Once everyone finished eating, they all cleared the table and after everything was cleaned up, Lisa set out the desserts. Apple and pumpkin pie and a platter of the gluten-free lemon bars. She noticed as she glanced out the window that Walter's car wasn't in his driveway. She hoped he was enjoying the day at his son's house. Rhett came up behind her, wrapped his arms around her, and gave her a quick kiss when she turned toward him.

"Thank you for a wonderful meal. Have I mentioned how thankful I am to be here with you?"

"You have. But I don't mind hearing it again." She smiled and kissed him back.

"Grampy, are you sleeping over?"

Travis smiled at the sweet sound of his daughter's voice as she threw herself at his father, demanding a hug.

"I think I will. Then we can eat turkey all day and stay up late reading books." His father scooped Sophie up and sat her on his lap. He and Travis were sitting at the kitchen table, snacking on cheese and crackers.

"Yay!"

Travis laughed. "Not too late." Sophie was a night owl and would stay up way past her bedtime if Travis allowed it. Maybe they could do a little later than usual tonight, though.

The turkey was just about ready. Travis had cooked it himself and ordered everything else already prepared—stuffing, mashed potatoes, butternut squash, Brussels sprouts and macaroni and cheese, which was Sophie's favorite. He was fine with cooking the turkey. He got a medium-sized one and followed the directions on how long to cook it. It also had a pop-out timer. When he took it out of the oven, it was golden brown and smelled pretty fantastic.

His father took on carving duty and once their plates were full, they gathered in the dining room, which hadn't been used once since he'd moved in. It was a pretty room with a great ocean view. It was a cool day and windy, so the waves were tipped with white as they raced toward the shore.

"Your view is almost as good as mine," his father teased him.

Travis smiled. "Almost. I'm pretty happy with how everything turned out. I'm thinking about getting a pool table for the basement. And I might add a theatre room and a wine cellar. Chase is going to swing by next week to work up an estimate."

"Didn't know you liked wine that much?" His father commented.

"I like it. Depends what I'm eating and who I'm with." His father was a beer drinker. "I thought about doing this before, but Beth knew we were anxious to get in. She suggested we live with it for a bit and then see what else we wanted to add."

His father nodded. "That seems like good advice. When we moved into our place, your mother thought she wanted a new kitchen immediately. But after using it for six months, she realized she liked the layout and just wanted new countertops and a coat of white paint on the cabinets."

"Have you heard from Kay?" Travis asked. His father was his usual cheerful self today, but he'd been quieter than usual for the first few days after Kay left.

"We've texted a few times. Sounds like she's having a good time in Charleston. She went out to a famous restaurant earlier today. Poogan's Porch. I looked it up on the internet. She said it was very good, and she made a friend, another lady her age. They're doing something this week, something food related."

"That sounds fun. Does she have any plans to come back to Nantucket?"

A sad look flashed across his father's face. "Not until the summer, I don't think."

"I like Kay!" Sophie said.

His father smiled. "She's a nice lady. I like her too."

"Summer will be here before you know it, Dad." Travis wondered if his father might be ready to start dating now. If not Kay, maybe someone else.

"I suppose it will. How are things going with Victoria? Last night was your third date, right?" His father had watched Sophie the night before for their weekly trivia night."

"Good, so far. You know she dumped me in high school? It was a long time ago, but it still makes me want to go real slow."

"I remember that. You two were just kids then, though. She seems like a good one. Her parents are good people and she seems reliable, has a steady job. Seems like she's maybe ready to settle down."

"She's looking to move out of her parents' place soon, and rent an apartment downtown. What do you think of that?" Travis worried that things seemed a little too good to be true with Victoria. His secret fear was a repeat of what happened in high school, that she'd suddenly change her mind about him.

"I like it. Shows she's not eager to jump into things too fast with you either, and that's a good thing. Also, if she rents a place, that's a commitment to be here for at least a year. Another good thing."

"Hmmm. I hadn't thought about it that way. You may have a point."

His father chuckled. "Sometimes I do. Don't sound so surprised."

Travis smiled. He looked around the table at his father and daughter and sighed with contentment. He was glad he'd made the decision to move home.

39

*V*ictoria put the word out among all her friends that she was starting a search for an apartment. Housing was always in short supply on Nantucket, and many times friends found rentals through other friends. There was nothing listed in the paper and she'd called all the area real estate offices and no one had anything suitable. Most of the available options were seasonal rentals only, and those prices were insane. There was almost nothing available year-round, and what was available was far out of her price range.

But a few days later, she got a call from Mia that the townhouse next to her might be available. Mia's friend Ben owned it, and it was a second home for him. His main residence was in Manhattan, and that's also where he worked most of the time. In the past, he'd been able to spend a lot of time working remotely from Nantucket, but Mia explained that he just took on a huge commercial development project that would require him to stay in Manhattan for the better part of the next year. So he was looking to sublet for a year.

Victoria had been to Mia and Izzy's place once and it was gorgeous and the location was ideal, right on the waterfront, by the wharf where the ferries came in. It was perfect, but she doubted that she could afford it. She had a good salary, but newspaper reporters were not highly paid.

Mia mentioned a number that was at the top of Victoria's range—but it was in the range. Victoria questioned it and Mia explained that Ben wanted to rent to someone he knew—or through friends, as this was his home and he wanted to make sure it was well taken care of. So it was worth it to him to ask for a lower rent to get someone trustworthy in there.

"Please tell him I'll take it," Victoria said. Mia laughed.

"Don't you want to see it first? I can show it to you after work if you want to stop by today?"

"Okay. I just don't want to lose out. I know I'm going to love it."

"You won't lose out. You're the only one I've told. Make sure you like it, and if you do, it's yours."

Victoria met Mia after work at her townhouse and they walked next door to Ben's unit. It was a mirror image of Mia's, with big windows overlooking the harbor and a kitchen that opened into a living room and two bedrooms. It was a perfect size. Ben had one of the bedrooms set up as a home office, with a sofa that pulled into a bed so it could also be a guest room. That worked well for Victoria, too.

"It's fully furnished, so you could move right in if you like it," Mia said.

"It's perfect." The decor was a little more masculine than Mia's unit—the sofa in the living room was a chocolate brown leather and the bedroom furniture was a dark pine. But otherwise, everything was modern and light. The kitchen was all-white cabinets which Victoria loved and the subway tile backsplash was ocean blue.

"Great. I'll let Ben know. He said you can move in as soon as December first, if you want."

That was less than a week away. It was sooner than she'd expected, but she didn't want to miss out on a great rental. "I have my checkbook. I can give you a check today."

"I'll send it off to Ben and just stop by here anytime after the first and I'll give you the keys. It will be fun having you as a neighbor!"

"I'm excited."

Victoria's parents were less enthused when she broke the news at dinner.

"Are you sure you want to do that, honey? We like having you around," her mother said,

"That's a pretty incredible spot," her father said. Her mother shot him a look, and he cleared his throat. "Of course we'll miss you, though. You really don't have to move out."

"It's been great being back home, but this was always meant to be temporary. This is a really great opportunity to be in my own waterfront place downtown—at least for a year." She grinned. "Maybe after that, I might come knocking on your door again. You never know."

"Well, you're always welcome. You know that. When will you move in? January or February?" Her mother asked.

"December actually. It's available right away. But I'm not going far. I'll still be over all the time to bug you both."

"Do you need to get any furniture for it?" Her father asked.

Victoria shook her head. "No, it's fully furnished. And you know the units? It's those gorgeous townhouses right on the wharf."

"It does sound lovely," her mother said.

"I'll have you both over for dinner as soon as I'm settled."

"I'll admit I had hopes that things might work out with Travis and eventually you'd just move from our place to his," her mother admitted.

"Travis is great. But it's way too soon to think about anything like that. He's not going to rush anything after what he went through with Sophie's mother. And I need to be really sure, too. But, I do like him!"

40

*L*ess than a week later, Victoria moved into the condo on the wharf. She'd started moving her things in that Thursday, which was December first and brought everything else over Friday after work. She didn't really have that much to move, mostly clothes and books and a few boxes of decorative stuff from her Boston apartment. When she'd moved home to Nantucket, she'd sold all her furniture and only took what was essential. She knew she was going to be living with her parents until the wedding and didn't want to deal with storing things that she didn't really need or want anymore.

So, between Friday night and Saturday morning, she was able to unpack and put just about everything away. Travis and Sophie were coming by in a bit to head out to the Nantucket Christmas Stroll. While she waited for them to arrive, Victoria did a final look through her book, which was all formatted and ready to upload to the online stores like Amazon, Apple, Google, and Barnes and Noble. Kate's editor had turned the book around in just under a week, and Victoria went through and accepted almost all the changes.

Taylor had volunteered to do a final proofread and had caught a few typos that the main editor had missed. Victoria was happy with how the cover had turned out. It was bright and pretty and she hoped it would attract the right readers to take a closer look. She took a deep breath, then closed her eyes and hit submit. The book was now on its way to be reviewed by the quality team at Amazon. As long as they didn't find any technical issues, the ebook and paperback would be available within a day or two.

Victoria then went through the same process at the other stores and once it was uploaded everywhere, she felt a sense of relief and excitement. She'd talked to both Kate and Marley about marketing ideas for the book and drew up a marketing plan. Kate had told her how to do a few small ads on Amazon and Facebook that would drive traffic to the online stores.

And Marley had given her tips for how to market for free with social media. Victoria was already on Facebook and set up new accounts with Instagram, Pinterest, and TikTok. She was kind of feeling her way through it all, but it was fun and she was excited to see if it might help actual book buyers to find her book.

A few minutes later, at a quarter to twelve, there was a knock on the door—Travis and Sophie had arrived.

Victoria let them in and Sophie ran to her and wrapped her arms around Victoria's leg and looked up at her. "Are you excited to go see Santa Claus, Victoria?"

"Of course I am. Are you?"

"I'm so excited. Let's go." Sophie grabbed her hand and tugged.

Travis laughed. "Not just yet, Soph. We need to see Victoria's new place first."

"I'll give you the quick grand tour and then we can head out." Victoria showed them around. Travis was impressed. "This place is great. Will be a great spot to watch the fourth of July fireworks."

Victoria grinned. "Thanks. I was thinking the same. I'll probably have people over then for a cookout. It's ages away, but I'm already looking forward to it." She grabbed her coat and hat. "I'm ready to go."

It was a short walk to Main Street, and they joined the crowds of people strolling along the famous cobblestone streets of Nantucket. Even the brick on the sidewalks was wavy and had a cobblestone effect. It was something Nantucket was known for, and Victoria loved the quaint, old-fashioned look.

At twelve sharp, they turned to face the waterfront to see Santa arrive by boat. The coast guard always brought him in that way. He climbed off the boat when it docked at the wharf and onto a vintage fire truck to parade down Main Street. Travis lifted Sophie onto his shoulders so she could get a good view of the truck and of Santa as he rode by.

They had such a fun day. All the store windows along Main Street and the side streets were decorated for Christmas. They strolled along and stopped in many of the stores, which all had special items for Christmas or were giving out cups of warm cider or cookies. There was a cookie decorating table and Sophie loved decorating her own gingerbread cookie. Victoria chose a snowman to decorate, and Travis went with Santa. Once they were satisfied with their cookies, they ate them as they walked along.

Travis noticed a sign for an ugly Christmas sweater contest happening later that afternoon and laughed. "Too bad we didn't know about that ahead of time. I have a hideous sweater I could have worn. My mother gave it to me years ago and I trot it out every Christmas at least once. Sophie loves it."

"I need a Christmas sweater too, daddy. So we can wear them next year!"

Travis smiled at her. "Maybe, honey. That sounds like a good idea."

"Victoria, you have to come too!" Sophie said excitedly.

Victoria smiled. "That does sound fun." And she meant it. She realized that being here next year at this time, with all of them in their ugly Christmas sweaters, was exactly where she hoped to be.

41

After spending the afternoon at the Christmas Stroll with Victoria, Travis picked up pizzas on the way home. His father was coming by for dinner and they were going to watch Christmas movies with Sophie. His father had twisted his ankle walking on the beach and wasn't up to joining them for the Stroll.

When he pulled into his driveway, Travis noticed Victoria's parents unloading groceries from their car. He went over to say hello while Sophie took his keys and raced to the front door to let herself in.

"How old is she?" Victoria's father asked.

"Four going on fourteen," Travis said.

"Did you have a nice time at the Stroll? Victoria said you were meeting her there?" Victoria's mother asked.

"We did. We stopped by her new place too. It's nice!"

"It is a lovely spot. It is quiet without her here, though," her mother admitted.

"It's funny but I never thought the two of you would actually get together," Victoria's father said.

"Oh? Why's that?" Travis assumed it was because they'd already dated years ago.

"Well, I just never thought she'd go for someone who had a kid. Victoria was never into babysitting or anything like that. I wasn't sure if she even wanted to have kids."

Victoria's mother shot her husband a look that shut him up quickly.

"Don't mind me. I'm just rambling. I think the two of you are great together."

Travis wasn't sure what to think. He looked at Victoria's mother. "Did Victoria actually tell you that she didn't want kids?"

"No, of course not. She once said she wasn't sure when she and Todd were dating. We assumed, of course, that eventually that would change."

"I see. Well, I just wanted to come over and say hello. Have a good night."

"You too, dear." Victoria's mother looked worried, and Travis shared her concern. What if her parents were right, and that was still how Victoria felt?

42

*K*ay enjoyed the rest of her time in Charleston. She loved the food and had her fill of shrimp and grits. It was slightly different everywhere she went, but always good. It was something she just never saw on menus in the Boston area. Her new friend that she met on Thanksgiving gave her a great recipe for it to try when she got home, though. They met up several times that following week for the food tour and cooking event, which was wonderful. It was a walking history tour followed by a cooking demonstration and wine tasting. They also went to a luncheon and garden tour on a different day. By the time her second week was up, Kay was looking forward to getting home. She was actually tired of going out to eat—something she didn't think would be possible.

When she got home to Arlington though, after a day or two, she started to feel somewhat restless again. It was so quiet there now with her friends gone. She supposed she could look for new activities to get involved with, maybe pick up an extra shift at the food pantry or take another class, maybe knitting this time or possibly watercolor painting. That was something she'd always wanted to try.

She kept herself busy around the house, finally what she'd put off doing for so long—going through her closets and donating all of Al's clothing to local thrift shops. Her closet seemed oddly empty once it was cleared out of his things. It made her sad. Everywhere she looked in her house, she saw Al. Getting rid of his clothes didn't change that much. She decided to head out for a long walk and get some exercise. Maybe the fresh air would clear her mind.

She headed outside and bundled up with her warmest hat, puffy coat, and mittens. It was clear but cold and a bit windy. But it was also sunny, and as she walked and felt the sun on her face, she began to relax and feel a bit less blue. She walked all around her neighborhood, which surrounded a pretty park. There was a playground there and as she walked by, she smiled at the young children on the swing set with their parents close by. She remembered those days fondly. It seemed like just yesterday and a million years ago at the same time.

"Hello, Kay. Did you have a nice trip?" Henry, her mailman for the past twenty years, slowed his truck to say hello.

"Great time, Henry, thanks. Tell Louise I said hello." His wife also volunteered at the food pantry.

Kay walked on and on for at least an hour before she felt ready to head home. As she reached her street, her cellphone rang. She didn't recognize the number, though it did look oddly familiar. She thought she had seen it before, somewhere.

"Is this Kay Johnson?" The caller asked.

"This is Kay."

"Kay, it's Ava from Dover Falls. I may have some very good news for you. Are you still interested in one of our units?"

Kay stopped walking. "Yes, I am. But I thought there was a long wait for them?"

"There usually is, but we just had several units open up at once. A few moved into assisted living and one went to memory care. There were a few people ahead of you, but one of them just signed a contract somewhere else. So, you're up next."

"When is it available?" Kay felt almost lightheaded at the unexpected good news.

"It's available now. We would just need to process your paperwork and handle the financial details. But that can be done in a few days if you wish to move forward. The available unit is just like the one your friend Ginny is in."

"I'm interested. What do you need from me?"

"I'll email you the paperwork and we can get things started. Congratulations, Kay! We look forward to seeing you soon."

Kay ended the call and walked the rest of the way home with a smile on her face. Fate had intervened, and she was meant to go back to Nantucket, for good. The blues she'd been feeling earlier were gone and a sense of blissful happiness took its place. She had a lot to do, though, before she could make the move. She needed to list her house with her friend Cathy's daughter, who was a realtor. And she needed to line up a mover. And go through all of her things again. She'd already done a lot of the clearing out by going through her closet. Now she needed to do the rest of the house and pack up all of her things.

Her first impulse was to text Walter to tell him the good news. But then she thought it might be more fun to wait until everything was confirmed and she was actually in her new home on Nantucket. Then she could go knock on Walter's door and see if he wanted to go for a walk on the beach. She couldn't wait to see the look on his face. And she'd be there for Christmas. Kay hadn't been looking forward to spending a second holiday alone.

43

*V*ictoria's book was officially on sale now and available on all online platforms. Sales were very slow, but Kate told her not to worry about that.

"Remember, no one knows who you are, so sales will be slow at first. Just keep getting the word out and the sales will come. And then word of mouth will help too, once people start reading and reviewing it," she'd said.

Victoria took everyone's advice and made some ads and even tried to make some TikTok videos as Marley had instructed. She posted a new video every day, trying all different kinds of videos—some of her talking about the book, others of pretty graphics, or quotes, fun music. So far, nothing was going even close to viral, but Marley told her to just keep at it.

"You know what video will capture people's attention. It just takes one to get the ball rolling. Especially with your genre. Once you get your author copies, be sure to post a video of you holding the book. That cover is so pretty, that might help a lot," Marley had advised.

The box of author copies arrived on Tuesday and when Victoria arrived home from work, they were waiting by her door. She took the box inside and set up a tripod with her phone camera to take a video of her opening the box and lifting out her paperbacks. This was called an 'unboxing' and was apparently a big thing on TikTok.

Once the camera was in place, Victoria took a deep breath and grabbed a knife to open the box. She was surprised that she was already feeling a bit emotional, as she wasn't usually overly emotional. But when she opened the box and saw her books inside, she instantly felt her eyes grow damp. She lifted one up and it was just perfect. The colors were so pretty, and the cover had a smooth feel to the matte finish. It was her book! That she wrote. She realized that she needed to say something to the camera. She smiled big.

"Here it is! My first book is a romantic comedy with a bit of spicy steam. I hope you love it!"

She turned the camera off and picked up her book again. It was so beautiful. It was hard to believe she'd created it herself. She needed to tell someone. The first person she thought of was Travis, and she wanted to give him a call, but something held her back. She hadn't heard from him since the Christmas Stroll, which she thought was a little odd. Usually, he checked in by now to say hello and confirm that he would go to trivia with them.

She decided to call her mother instead and told her about it.

"Honey, that's so exciting. I can't wait to see it. What are you doing for dinner?"

"No plans. I was going to heat up some soup."

"Why don't you come here instead? I just made a big tray of lasagna. You can bring me your book to look at. Your father will want to see it too."

Victoria laughed. "I'll bring one for you. I ordered a bunch. And lasagna sounds great."

After dinner with her parents, Victoria was in a great mood and decided to go say hello to Travis before she headed home. She knocked on his front door and was surprised that he didn't seem happy to see her.

"This is a surprise," he said.

"I'm sorry. Am I catching you in the middle of something? I just had dinner with my parents and we were celebrating. I just got copies of my book in the mail."

"That's great, congrats." Travis stepped outside and closed the door behind him. Something was up. It was strange that instead of inviting her in, he'd shut the door behind him, as if he didn't want Sophie to know that Victoria was there.

"I suppose this is better that you came by, actually. I was planning to call you tomorrow. I'm not going to be able to make it to trivia."

"Oh, that's too bad." Victoria smiled. "Not a big deal, though. You can come next week."

He shook his head. "I don't think that's a good idea." He stayed quiet for a moment before finally saying, "You know that Sophie is the most important thing in my world?"

She nodded. "Yes, of course she is."

"Well, I had a chat with your parents yesterday and your father let it slip that he was surprised we were dating, given that you've never been all that into kids."

Victoria's heart sank. "He actually said that?"

"That was the gist of it, yeah. And your mother confirmed it."

"She did? I mean, I used to feel that way, sure. I just never thought much about having kids."

"He said you never babysat."

"I didn't. I wasn't into dolls either. I admit it. And I wasn't eager to have kids. Like it wasn't something I always dreamed about, the way some girls do."

Travis nodded and waited for her to continue.

"But that doesn't mean I'm not interested now. Or that I don't love spending time with Sophie."

He looked sad. "Victoria, I think you're great. I really do. But I'm just not sure we're on the same path here. You just got your own place and have a job you love. You might never want kids and probably never thought about dating someone that already has them. And that's okay. It just means that we're better off as friends."

"As friends?"

"Yeah. But probably not for a while. I don't want to confuse Sophie and honestly, it will be too hard for me too."

Victoria tried again. "Travis, I swear to you, that isn't how I feel now. I'm fine with kids, especially Sophie."

Travis hesitated for a moment, then shook his head sadly. "I can't take the chance that you might change your mind and dump us—dump me, again."

"There's nothing I can say that will change your mind?" Victoria's voice broke as her eyes welled up.

And Travis looked just as miserable. "I'm sorry, Victoria."

She turned to go, and the tears fell. It wasn't until she

got into her car though, that the sobs came, fast and hard, and she cried like she hadn't cried in years. She drove home slowly, let herself into her new condo and collapsed on her sofa, feeling utterly and totally alone and sadder even than she'd felt after Todd ended things.

44

*V*ictoria felt like skipping trivia that week, but Taylor wouldn't let her. She'd filled Taylor in that morning when they'd both arrived in the office. Taylor listened sympathetically and then offered her two cents.

"I understand his concern. Especially after what happened with his wife and with the two of you in high school. But he still might come around once he really thinks this through. You're not the same person he knew in high school. And you're nothing like his wife. People change. You did, after all, tell me that you wanted nothing to do with him because he had a kid—but you just hadn't really been around them before."

"That's true. I didn't really know what I wanted. Sophie is adorable. She's easy to be around. I don't know why Travis can't just believe me." Victoria understood his concern, but it was frustrating that he couldn't trust that her feelings had changed.

"And staying home tonight is silly. What are you going

to do, just mope, eat ice cream and watch Hallmark movies?"

That was exactly what Victoria had planned.

"I like Hallmark movies," she said.

"Come out with your friends and get your mind off of it. No sense staying home and feeling sad. Come have fun."

"All right. I told Beth I'd give her a copy of my book tonight anyway, so I guess I have to go."

"Did you tell her about Travis?" Taylor asked.

"I filled her in, yeah. She agrees with you. She thinks he might just need some time, that all is not lost yet."

Victoria had fun at trivia and except for an initial wave of sadness that Travis wasn't there with them, she managed to get her mind off of it and enjoy the night out with her friends.

She handed Beth a copy of her book when she and Chase arrived.

"I wanted you to have a signed copy, to thank you for being an early reader," Victoria said.

"Oh, you didn't have to do that." Beth happily took the paperback, ran her fingers over it and flipped it over to see the design on the back cover. "It's so pretty. Thank you! It will look gorgeous on my bookshelf."

A little while later, Beth turned to her when the others weren't paying attention and spoke softly. "I'm so sorry about Travis. We're actually seeing him tomorrow. Chase and I are going to his place to talk about a new project he wants us to work on. I wish I could do something to help."

"Thanks. There's really nothing you can do. I wish there was."

"Well, try to get your mind off it. Let's just have fun tonight."

Victoria smiled. "That's the plan!"

They didn't win, but they did come in a respectful second place, which also gave them a $15 gift card. Blake was very happy about that and insisted on buying a round for all of them. Victoria happily accepted, as she wasn't in a hurry to go home. And now that she lived downtown, she could just walk home in about five minutes. Another advantage of her new residence—she loved being able to walk to work.

As they walked out, Victoria overheard a woman in front of them chatting to her friend. "I heard Travis Sturgess is living on Nantucket now. Maybe we'll run into him here. Someone said they saw him here playing trivia."

"Well, we'll have to come again next week," her friend said. Both women were attractive and about Victoria's age. The conversation instantly depressed her. Travis wouldn't have any trouble moving on. As hard as it might be, she should try to do the same, instead of hoping he might change his mind.

45

*B*eth and Chase met Travis at his house the next morning at ten. The house was quiet when Travis opened the door. Beth expected to hear or see Sophie running around. When she didn't appear after a few minutes, she asked about her.

"She's with my dad for the morning. He has her most days, at least for the morning, so I can focus and get work done."

Travis led them down to his partially finished basement. He'd left it with Chase that he wanted to get back to him about what he wanted to do with the basement and wanted to move in first and then decide.

"How are you liking it so far?" Chase asked.

Travis grinned. "It's great. Sophie and I love it here. I wanted to give it a little time to figure out what I will actually use down here. I think I want to do a walk-in wine cellar, a sauna, and a home theater room."

Chase nodded. "What do you have in mind for the theater area?"

Travis showed him where he wanted it to go. "I'm thinking two rows of built in reclining seats, with table areas on either side and a thick plush carpet in case Sophie and her friends want to lie on the floor."

"What about painting the walls of just this section a much darker color, so it will seem to recess even more into the darkness for the movie?" Beth suggested. She'd seen that done, and it looked really cool.

Travis considered the idea and nodded. "I like it. Let's do that."

Chase and Travis talked specifics on materials while Beth walked around the room and took some measurements of the area he wanted for the wine cellar.

"How long have you been into wine, Travis?" She asked when he and Chase walked over to join her.

"I got into it in California. We lived near wine country. I've gone to so many wineries and tasting rooms. My dad is a beer drinker so I haven't had as much wine since I've been back here, but I've been drinking it again since I started dating Victoria." He hesitated for a moment. "I suppose she updated you?"

Beth nodded. "She did. I'm sorry to hear it."

Chase sensed the awkwardness and changed the subject. "Travis, we can get back to you later today with an estimate. Beth and I will work on it once we get back to the office and we'll shoot you an email."

Travis looked relieved. "Great. Thanks for coming out here, you guys."

They went back upstairs and Beth whispered to Chase, "When we get to the door, walk ahead of me. I want to talk to Travis for a minute."

Chase raised his eyebrows and whispered back, "are you sure that's a good idea?"

"I'm sure."

Chase shook Travis' hand when they reached the door. "We'll talk to you soon." He strode toward the truck and Beth hung back.

"Travis, can I talk to you for a second?"

"Sure. What's up?"

"Well, I don't want to get in the middle of anything, but I just have a question for you. Have you read Victoria's book?"

"Her book? No. She said it was just published."

Beth reached into her oversized tote bag and pulled out the signed paperback that Victoria had given her. She handed it to Travis.

"That's my copy, so I need it back. But I've already read it. I think you should, too. You haven't known Victoria all that long. I know you dated for two seconds in high school, but that was a million years ago. My point is you think you know her, based on that and what her parents said—but you don't. Not really. If you read her book, well, you'll know how she really feels. That book is fiction. But on many levels, it's real. It's Victoria. Do you care about her at all?"

"Of course I do." Travis looked stunned at Beth's outburst.

"Then just read it." She smiled sweetly. "And check your email for that estimate later today."

46

The next week was a flurry of activity for Kay. She met with the realtor and arranged to have her house put on the market the day after she left for Nantucket. The movers were coming in the morning and Kay had an early afternoon reservation on the slow ferry. She booked a cleaner to come that same day and the realtor promised to make sure the house was locked up after they left.

It all happened so fast that Kay was too busy to feel sad about leaving her home of so many years. Occasionally, as she packed up special pictures of her and Al or childhood pictures of Tony, she would feel a pang of sadness and loss. But it passed quickly. Kay had grieved for her husband and now she was ready to move into her new life, her new community, on Nantucket.

The movers came at eight sharp on moving day. By the time everyone arrived at Dover Falls, it was late afternoon and it took them a while to move everything in, and to get Kay's bed set up. By the time they left, it was almost five.

Kay unpacked as much as she could and spent most of the evening putting things away and setting up her new home. She only stopped once to take a quick break and eat a turkey sandwich that she'd brought with her. Finally, at a little past ten, she found the box that had her sheets, made her bed and fell into it, exhausted but happy.

Kay woke early the next day, feeling well rested and excited for what she had planned. She showered and changed and drove herself to The Corner Table for a coffee and a scone. It was almost nine, about the time she used to take her morning beach walks when she stayed at the inn. She drove there, parked at the inn, and walked down to the beach.

She walked up to the lighthouse and back, her usual walk. And on the way back, she slowed when she got to Walter's house and made her way towards his steps. She'd planned to knock on his door and surprise him, but as she reached the top step, his door flew open and Walter stepped outside.

"Kay? Is that really you? I thought my eyes were playing tricks on me. I was sitting by the window, sipping my coffee and I saw this woman go by, heading toward the lighthouse, and she looked so much like you. I didn't really think it was you, though."

Kay took a step forward. "It's me, Walter. I'm back. For good this time."

Walter's smile lit up his face. "Tell me more."

She laughed. "Charleston was great, but I was sorry that I didn't stay here for Thanksgiving. I missed everyone. When I got home to Arlington, I missed you all even more. My friends are gone now, moved out of state. It's just not the same." She told him about Ginny and the opening at Dover Falls.

"So it just seemed meant to be. I have new friends here that feel like family."

Walter took a step closer and pulled her in for a hug. "You have no idea how much I missed you."

Kay squeezed him tight and when they pulled back, she looked him in the eye and smiled. "I really missed you, too."

Walter leaned in and kissed her, taking her totally by surprise. It was a quick kiss, and he looked pleased with himself when he finished. "I hope you don't mind, but I've been wanting to do that since the night we went to dinner and I kicked myself that I was too chicken to do it then."

Kay felt a rush of happiness. "Well, I'm glad you did it now. I think it's the right time for both of us." She leaned forward and kissed him back, and this time, they both let the kiss linger.

"You know part of me wants to ask you to move right in, but it's probably too soon for that, I suppose?" He had a mischievous gleam in his eyes.

Kay laughed. "Yes, Walter. Remember you told your son it's a good idea to be with someone for a full calendar year before you get serious? I think that is good advice for anyone, even us."

Walter grinned. "I can wait. I'm just so glad you're here. Are you ready for a cup of coffee?"

"I am." She followed him inside and he poured her a cup and she took it to her usual chair by the window. Walter sat next to her in his favorite chair. They sipped their coffee and looked out the window and all was well with their world.

47

After Sophie went to bed, Travis picked up the book that Beth had given him. Victoria's book. He glanced at the back blurb. It was a romantic comedy about a driven and highly competitive woman who didn't think she wanted kids who falls for her high school sweetheart, who is a divorced single father.

He opened the book and started reading. And stayed up until he finished the book at a little after two am. His mind swirled. Beth had said the book was the real Victoria, that it represented how she felt. If that was true, then he needed to talk to her.

Marley called Victoria a few minutes after she got home from work. She'd just made herself a cup of lemon green tea and settled on her living room sofa with her laptop. She was about to check her book sales and make a new video for TikTok.

"Can you chat for a minute?" Marley asked.

"Sure, perfect timing. I just got home a few minutes ago."

"Great. Have you checked your sales yet today?"

"No, not yet, why? I was just about to do that."

"I'm curious if you might have a spike in sales. Your unboxing video is trending."

"It is?" It hadn't gotten much attention when Victoria uploaded it a few days ago.

"Someone that read your book found that video and raved about it on TikTok. And it's a BookTok influencer with almost a million followers. She only did it a few hours ago, but it's getting a ton of comments and likes and shares. That usually translates to sales."

"That's awesome! I'll check now." Victoria pulled up her sales page on Amazon and almost dropped her phone. "I've had over two hundred sales! I usually only have two or three in a day!"

"Excellent. It's probably going to keep spiking for a while. That will drive your book's rank up too, which will then make it more visible and lead to more sales."

"And this is just because that one person shared my TikTok video?" Victoria was in awe.

"Yes. That's how powerful TikTok can be. You'll probably see an increase in views on some of your other videos now and more followers. I'd get a new video up as soon as possible to keep it going."

"I will. I was about to do that when you called."

"Good! Keep me posted. And congrats."

"Thank you!" Victoria ended the call and looked up the video that Marley had mentioned. The reader raved about Victoria's book and suggested that all of her followers read it immediately. It was a surreal moment to imagine that people were actually reading her book and liking it enough to tell others to read it, too.

Victoria spent the next half hour making another video, with fun music and quotes from the book that readers had highlighted. She had just finished the video and was uploading it on TikTok when there was a knock at the front door. She figured it was probably an Amazon delivery person as she wasn't expecting anyone and she had ordered a few things online. But when she opened the door, it was Travis, holding a copy of her book.

"Hey there. Could I come in? I'm not interrupting anything?" he asked,

"No, come in. Do you want something to drink?"

He shook his head. "No, I just have a few questions. Beth gave me her copy of your book—just to borrow, she said she needed it back. But she thought I should read it."

"You read my book?" That surprised her.

He nodded. "I did. It was very well written. Not my usual type of thing, but it was good." He hesitated. "Beth also said that I didn't really know you. But that the book is you. Is that true?"

"Is what true?" Victoria was a little confused by what exactly he was asking.

He opened the book and found the page he had bookmarked.

"Anna says, 'I never thought much about having kids. I never wanted to babysit, and I never dreamed of being a mother. I never thought about it the way I thought about having a successful career and an exciting life. I was always so competitive and driven and just focused on what I wanted. So when I met him again, after not seeing him since high school and discovered he had a young child, I immediately put him into a friends only bucket."

Victoria sighed. "Yes, that's how I felt at the time. But my feelings changed. I told you that."

"You did. But you can understand how that was hard for me to believe? I felt like you just said that in the moment, and maybe it wasn't how you really felt."

"Well, you were wrong. I care about both of you."

Travis opened the book to another page and read aloud, "As I spent time with him and his daughter, I realized that I liked being around some children, after all. And I started to fall in love with both of them. I couldn't imagine him without her or my life without both of them in it. But I don't know if he will ever believe me or if he can get past how I used to feel to see how I truly feel now. They are both so important to me and I'm afraid that I've lost them."

He paused for a moment. "Is that all true, too?"

Victoria nodded. "Yes, it's true. It's fiction, but Anna is based on me and her feelings are my feelings. It's very real."

"So what do we do about this?" Travis still looked confused, but she sensed there was a spark of hope there, too.

"Why don't we take your father's advice?"

"What advice is that?"

"You once told me that he thought you married Kacey too soon and that you should spend four seasons with someone before making such a big decision. I'm sure of how I feel, but I still think that's good advice. I signed a year lease, so let's take this year to get to know each other better—who we are now, not who we were and build on that. I adore your daughter, and you. And I'm not going anywhere."

He grinned. "I'm pretty crazy about you, too. You promise not to dump me for the star quarterback?"

She laughed. "I like to think I'm a little older and wiser now."

Travis pulled her close and she wrapped her arms around him. He touched his lips to hers and she leaned in for his kiss. When they pulled back, his eyes met hers, and they both smiled. "So, I guess we're back together now?" He said softly.

"I guess so."

"My dad and Kay are watching Sophie and it's Scrabble night. He ordered pizzas and I have to pick them up along the way. He also ordered me to bring you back with me… are you in?"

She laughed again. "Depends. What kind of pizza did you get?"

"Pepperoni and cheese."

"Then I'm in."

EPILOGUE

*L*isa glanced out the kitchen window and smiled at the sight of the fat, fluffy snowflakes swirling in the air. It was the perfect kind of snow—called ocean effect—light snow flurries that looked pretty coming down, but the winds blew it out to sea instead of onto the ground.

There was a possibility of a white Christmas but there would be no shoveling or plowing needed if the forecast was right and it didn't collect too much.

"I hope I have enough food." Lisa surveyed the kitchen counter and island where she'd set out a platter of sliced cheeses, hard salami, roasted nuts and crackers. She'd made her friend Andrew's clam dip, which was amazing. Andrew was a former chef, and he'd shared quite a few great recipes with her and this one was always a crowd pleaser.

"You always have plenty of food. And the kids are bringing more," Rhett said. "I'm pouring a glass of cabernet. Are you ready for one?"

She nodded. Their guests would be arriving at any

moment. Every year, Lisa hosted an open house on the afternoon of Christmas Eve for their family and friends. Kate was bringing shrimp cocktail from her husband, Jack's family business, Trattel Seafood. Kristen said she was going to make brownies Ina Garten's way. Lisa looked up that recipe and couldn't wait to try them—the recipe called for two pounds of chocolate and a lot of butter.

Lisa also had a tray of stuffed mushrooms in the oven and a big pot of Lobster Newburg on the stove with toast cups to serve it in. Rhett handed her a glass of wine, and she relaxed and took a small sip. "I suppose we do have enough," she agreed.

"Although that Lobster Newburg smells so good, you might have to shoo me away from it," Rhett said.

Lisa laughed. "It is good, and I made double the amount I thought we'd need, so maybe we'll have some leftovers."

At four sharp, the front door opened and people began arriving. Kate and the rest of Lisa's family were the first to enter. Followed soon after by Paige, Sue, Marley, and their partners. Kay came next, with Walter, his son Travis, granddaughter Sophie, and Travis's girlfriend, Victoria.

Everyone helped themselves to wine or a cocktail and they spent the next few hours eating, drinking and being very merry. Lisa was glad to see that there was plenty of food and, as usual, the Lobster Newburg was a big hit. She was glad that she'd made more this year.

"Lisa, this is so good. I might have to get the recipe from you," Kay said. They were chatting in the kitchen and Lisa was thrilled to see how happy Kay was since she'd moved to Nantucket. She was glad for her that she'd found a new friend and more with Walter and that she liked it at Dover Falls.

"I'm happy to give you the recipe. Are you cooking much these days?"

Kay shook her head. "No, not really. I go to the restaurant at Dover Falls usually, or eat at Walter's. But I do miss cooking a little and thought it might be nice to have Walter over for dinner one night—maybe New Year's eve. He told me earlier how much he loves your Lobster Newburg."

"Well, then you have to make it for him. I'm so glad you decided to come back here. We were thinking of you on Thanksgiving and missed you."

"Thank you. I'm glad this worked out, and I was able to get back in time for Christmas. I wasn't looking forward to being by myself again."

"I haven't seen Walter look this happy in a long time, either," Lisa said.

Kay nodded. "He loves having his family around him."

Lisa smiled. "And you."

"Maybe that, too! I honestly never expected this when I came to Nantucket for a long vacation. I've found a new community here, and it feels like it's where I am supposed to be."

Lisa gave her a hug. "You are definitely where you are supposed to be."

Beth stopped over to say hello and Lisa asked her about the property she and Chase had just bought and what her plans were for it.

"It's a terrifying house—really an awful first impression. It's in horrible shape. It's been empty for several years and has fallen into a bad state. One wall is caving in and the roof is full of holes." It didn't sound like the usual kind of house that Beth was drawn to.

"But you see promise in it?" Lisa asked.

"Aside from the roof and that one wall, the rest of it is cosmetic stuff. But it looks so bad that it scared most people off. The bones of the house are pretty good and it's on a hill, so it has potential for great ocean views."

Lisa was intrigued. "What will you do to it?"

"Chase will repair the roof and shore up the sagging wall first, replacing the rotting wood with all new. Then we're going to change the layout a bit and open it up from a lot of small, choppy rooms to several bigger open-concept ones. And we're going to add more sliders and big windows to let in the light and open up the views."

"And then you'll flip it?" Lisa assumed that was the plan.

"We might keep this one actually, and do short-term summer rentals with it. It's less than a half-mile from the beach, so that's an easy walk."

"And you could get top-dollar for it." There was always a shortage of rentals that close to the beach. They wouldn't have any trouble renting it out.

Beth nodded. "We still may end up selling it, but we thought it could be smart to hold it for a few years and let it appreciate even more while we earn income from renting."

That sounded smart to Lisa. "Was this your idea or Chase's?" Beth was the one that had urged Chase to take on his first flip-house and now they did them regularly.

"Mine. But Chase thought it would be a good experiment to try—renting instead of selling immediately."

"You two make a good team," Lisa said.

"Thanks." Beth spotted Victoria and waved her over. "I got your email about the book launch party. That sounds so fun. Chase and I will definitely be there."

"Great, it should be fun, hopefully," Victoria said. She glanced at Lisa. "I hope you and Rhett can make it too. I just sent all the invitations out yesterday by email."

"I got it this morning. We'll be there. I still need to read your book. I'll buy one at your launch. My daughters have been raving about it."

"Thank you. I'm glad the date seems to work for everyone so far. I wasn't sure about that since it is New Year's eve, but it's in the afternoon, so people can still go to dinner or New Year's parties or whatever they want."

"That will probably be it for us. We'll come home and have a quiet night after. Rhett and I are looking forward to that," Lisa said.

"How are sales going for the book?" Beth asked.

"Surprisingly well, I think. It's not a best seller of course or anything close to it, but the sales seem to be steadily increasing and the reviews are mostly good. TikTok has definitely helped to get the word out."

"I'm actually seeing it help my mysteries a little too." Kate walked over in time to hear Victoria's comment. She added a few shrimp onto her plate and dunked one in cocktail sauce before eating it.

"That's great, honey," Lisa said.

Marley walked over and Lisa lifted her glass in her direction. "I think we should toast to Marley and her marketing magic. My sales are up too, thanks to those silly videos."

Marley laughed. "It's been fun helping you all."

A moment later, Travis joined them and put his arm around Victoria and she leaned into him. His daughter was in the other room with the other children. They were all gathered around Walter, who was wearing a Santa hat and reading them a Christmas story.

"How are you liking your new place? Kate told me it's right next to Mia's townhouse. Those are lovely," Lisa said.

Victoria smiled. "I love it. It's really a great spot and I can walk to work from there."

"I liked it better when she lived next door," Travis teased, then added. "Just kidding. It's really a great place."

"Well, I'm happy for both of you." The two of them looked so happy together and Lisa suspected that it wouldn't be long before they were engaged and eventually Victoria would move into Travis's house.

She looked around the room and sighed with contentment. This was one of her favorite events, when all of her friends and family gathered at her house. A streetlight was visible from the big living room window and cast a glow on the snow that was still dancing in the air. It was a magical sight, and Lisa looked forward to a merry and white Christmas.

*T*hank you so much for reading **Nantucket Homes!**

Have you preordered The Bookshop by the Bay yet? I'm so excited for you to read this book. It's about mothers and daughters, a beloved bookshop in Chatham, Cape Cod and a summer of second chances and new possibilities.

My most recent book is **Gilded Girl**. It's a rags-to-riches Cinderella story set in the Gilded Age.

Lastly, if you are on Facebook but not yet in my Pamela Kelley Facebook Reader Group, please join us. It's a fun, friendly group and I often do special giveaways and share updates and cover and story information there.

ACKNOWLEDGMENTS

A huge thank you to my early readers and proofreaders, Jane Barbagallo, Taylor Barbagallo, Amy Petrowich, Laura Horan and Cindy Tahse.

ABOUT THE AUTHOR

Pamela M. Kelley is a USA Today and Wall Street Journal bestselling author of women's fiction, family sagas, and suspense. Readers often describe her books as feel-good reads with people you'd want as friends.

She lives in a historic seaside town near Cape Cod and just south of Boston. She has always been an avid reader of women's fiction, romance, mysteries, thrillers and cook books. There's also a good chance you might get hungry when you read her books as she is a foodie, and is also working on a cookbook.